W9-BMB-957

D

ANGEL
WINGS

ALSO BY HOWARD KAMINSKY

AS BROOKS STANWOOD
The Glow
The Seventh Child

AS ARTHUR REID
The Storyteller

WITH SUSAN KAMINSKY
Talent
The Twelve

WITH ALEXANDRA PENNEY
Magic Words
Magic Words at Work

ANGEL WINGS

a novel by

HOWARD KAMINSKY

THOMAS & MERCER

The characters and events portrayed in this book are fictitious. Any similarity to real persons, living or dead, is coincidental and not intended by the author.

Text copyright © 2013 Howard Kaminsky
All rights reserved.

Printed in the United States of America.

No part of this book may be reproduced, or stored in a retrieval system, or transmitted in any form or by any means, electronic, mechanical, photocopying, recording, or otherwise, without express written permission of the publisher.

Published by Thomas & Mercer
P.O. Box 400818
Las Vegas, NV 89140

ISBN-13: 9781611098877
ISBN-10: 1611098874
Library of Congress Control Number: 2012950073

For Susan. Always.

O Woman! lovely Woman! Nature made thee
To temper man: we had been brutes without you.
Angels are painted fair, to look like you.

* * *

—Thomas Otway, *Venice Preserved* (1682), Act I, Scene I

BEFORE

HE ALWAYS *kept the thermostat in the basement room set at sixty-two degrees. He worked better when it was cool. Just like Sir Laurence Olivier, he thought, smiling. Olivier was known for always telling the stage manager to make sure the theater was chilly to keep the audience awake. The room was small, and the only window, facing the backyard, was spray-painted black on the inside. One wall had floor-to-ceiling shelves that held all the materials he needed to do his work. A large, circular aluminum light fixture with six 100–watt bulbs was suspended over a long pine table covered in latex. There was no other furniture in the room.*

He worked slowly and carefully. It had to be just right. As usual, he had the Glenn Gould version of The Goldberg Variations *playing. The volume was low, but he could still hear Gould humming along with the music. God, he was good.*

He cut the hair first. He always had a talent for it. He remembered cutting his sister's hair when he was a kid. After that he applied the powder. He had experimented with brushes made by Lancôme, Clinique, and Bobbi Brown but found that using a man's shaving brush made of badger was the best. Then he started on the eyebrows and lashes. Less is more, he whispered to himself. The lips he saved for last. Just the lightest touch with the lipstick. Estée Lauder #168. Divine Wine. He stepped back from the table and studied his efforts. A little more powder was needed on the brow. He then reached for a stick of charcoal. Slowly, at the middle of the forehead, he drew a cross. Now it was perfect. He leaned down and lightly kissed the woman on the cheek. Her skin was as dry as a drumskin. He saw that his lips had made a mark. He picked up the powder brush again.

He reached over to a small table for two pieces of folded yellow fabric. They were made of the same material as the wrapping that enclosed the body; only its blue color was different. He had drawn the outline of wings with a pen on the yellow fabric and then carefully cut them out with a large pair of pinking scissors. He pushed one wing under the woman's right shoulder and held it out, away from the body. The effect was perfect.

The woman on the table was young, midtwenties at the most. She had lived a short and hard life. Now, after his transformation, she looked fresh, beautiful, and, yes, almost virginal. She had become an angel. She was ready to take her place in the firmament. The ugliness of her life was now behind her. He had transformed her into a pure, celestial being. He folded her hands across her chest and then switched off the light.

CHAPTER ONE

EDDIE MOTT, aka the Flea, is a piece of dirt. Bottom-of-the-shoe variety. But every so often he had proven to be very useful dirt for us. Also, and maybe this came from being on the force for almost ten years, I kind of liked him. The Flea called that morning and asked my partner, Alex, to meet him in a coffeehouse across from the Brown campus.

"What you got, Flea?" Alex asked him.

"Gold. Pure gold, Detective Larch."

"How about a hint?"

"It'll only cost you an espresso. And I guarantee you'll love it. If you don't, I'll pay."

"You're looking good, Flea," said Alex as he and I sat down in the booth. "You look like you've lost quite a few pounds. Weight Watchers?"

"Nah, just good nutrition. I'm down almost forty-five pounds. Getting in shape for the big one."

"The big one?" I asked.

"The Nathan's Hot Dog Eating Contest in Coney Island. It's the Everest for competitive eaters. That's what I'm training for."

"What the hell is competitive eating?"

"It's big, Detective Martell. You can make some real money at it. I'm surprised you haven't heard of it. Even CNN covers the Nathan's event."

Now, the Flea generally weighed somewhere between 350 and 400 pounds, so his recent weight loss didn't exactly make him look like he could get into a suit off the rack, but I had to admit there was a difference. Alex and I always referred to the Flea as a general practitioner: he did a little fencing, some loan sharking, occasional credit card scams, even some pimping on the side. He never hurt anyone and hadn't been inside for any significant time. But now he had a problem. He had been found guilty of possessing 193 stolen DVD players a week before. He was due to be sentenced next month. Serious time was definitely on the horizon. But first we had to hear about competitive eating.

"I'm totally committed to this. Every morning I wake up at six and go to the gym. I spend two hours there. I do twenty-nine miles on an exercise bike and then walk a mile on the indoor track. Then, two weeks before a big contest, I eat a head of boiled cabbage every day and later drink two gallons of water as fast as I can. I came in third last month in a shrimp-eating contest in St. Louis. I did three pounds, six ounces in eleven minutes."

"That's impressive," said Alex. "But if I were you, I'd add eating Judge Rubin's gavel to your menu. I hear he's going to hand you some heavy time, Flea."

"That's why I asked you guys to meet me here. I need you two to talk to him and that prick assistant DA, Minichiello. You have to get them to give me a break."

"We need some motivation. What do you have for us?" asked Alex.

"Like I told you, this is dynamite. Your Captain Kitty will cream over it. So will Rubin and Minichiello."

"Okay. You got our attention, Flea," I said. "Lay it out."

"You guys know who Bernie Sands is?"

We nodded. Sands was the worst slumlord in Providence. As bad as they come. A scumbag's scumbag. We had almost nailed him on an arson rap a few years before, but missed. Getting Sands would bring on an early Christmas.

"He came to me last month to help him get the last two tenants out of a building of his over on Gurney Street. He wants to condo it. The first one, a graduate student at Brown, was easy. A word or two with him and then a bottle of ammonia tossed through his window, and he was out of there. Left like he was late for class. Piece of cake. The other one was tougher. A whole other story. Like cracking a walnut with just your fingers. Name's Molly Juste. Maybe thirty. Good looking, with a body that could get her a page or two in that Victoria's Secret catalog. Wants to be an actress but keeps her head above water by waitressing at some expensive restaurant on the other side of the river. I tried everything on her, but she won't budge. So finally I told Sands to get another boy. Getting rough is not my thing. That's when he upped the game. Offered me $15,000 to get rid of her any way I wanted. 'Do you understand what you're saying?' I asked him. 'Kill the bitch,' he tells me. 'But make it look like an accident.' So I came up with the idea of giving her a hot shot. Make it look like she OD'd. Sands loved it."

"When are you supposed to do this?" I asked.

"I told him I'd do it after I get back from a pizza-eating contest this weekend in Scranton. I leave tomorrow."

I looked over at Alex. He was wearing a wide-screen version of his killer smile. All the ladies love it.

"Think you'll be able to help me?"

"If you do your part, really do it, Detective Larch and I would be more than happy to tell them what a big help you've been to us and the city of Providence."

"That's great, Detective."

"We'll call you soon, Flea," I said. "Good luck with the pizzas."

"And watch out for the anchovies," added Alex.

CHAPTER TWO

THE OFFICE was silent, except for an occasional scratch from one of the cats working at the carpet-covered post in the corner. We sat across from Captain Kitty, who was feverishly working her computer, as focused as a concert pianist. Neither of us said a word. We had just laid out our plan to set up Bernie Sands, and now we needed her okay to go ahead. She didn't fool us with her computer action. We'd seen it before at times like this. It was her standard cover while making her mind up about something.

Catherine Berkowitz was the highest-ranked woman on the Providence police force. She was about fifty, wore too much makeup, and was smart (she once won $62,000 on *Jeopardy*) and very short. We called her Captain Kitty but never to her face. Someone must have liked her way back then, because she got a height waiver without having to go to the courts. Even now she was as sensitive about her shortness as other women are about their age. The Captain claimed to be five feet two, but even her cats didn't believe it.

She had two passions: the police department and her four cats, Rico, Felony, Cuffs, and Miranda. She always had two in the office. Today it was Miranda and Rico. Rico was perched on top of a bookcase, the tallest piece of furniture in the office, examining his tail with the concentration of a diamond cutter looking for a flaw. Miranda, when she finally finished her scratching, ignored Rico and jumped onto Alex's lap.

"She likes either your cologne," I whispered, "or maybe the way your hair falls over your collar."

"Both," said Alex, with a wink. "But mainly I think she smells my cat, Samantha. That's what you and Linda need. A good cat. It'll change your life. If you don't believe me, just ask our Captain."

Alex was good looking and knew it. He was vain and not above enjoying even the attentions of a cat. For years I had called him Comb because he couldn't pass a mirror without combing his hair. I finally got him to stop, but he still gave his hair—fine, blond, and worn long—a pat whenever he passed a mirror. He was a real ladies' man and swore he had no plans to marry. Ever. I was his opposite in looks: dark hair, the complexion of a Navajo, with a better build and an intriguing scar that snaked down my jawbone. It was an old diving injury, but I liked to let people think that I might have gotten it in a dark alley early on. We had been partners for almost six years and knew each other so well we could almost, as the cliché goes, complete each other's sentences.

"Boys," said the Captain, looking up from her computer and raising her voice, "I've got a beauty for you today. *Agelast. A-g-e-l-a-s-t*. Well?"

"Don't have a clue," said Alex, while I nodded in agreement. We recognized the source, a website named A Word A Day, which specialized in obscure, off-the-wall words. The Captain was devoted to it.

"The word means 'someone who cannot laugh.' I'm going to quiz you tomorrow, so don't forget it. I'll want a sentence from both of you using it."

"Oh, Captain, you wouldn't do that, would you?" I asked with a mock groan. It was part of the ritual.

"I'm only joking," she said, pausing to pet Rico, now down from the bookcase, before continuing. "Let's get serious. I like your idea. Shows a lot more imagination than I usually expect from you two."

We talked a bit more about where, when, and how to execute the plan, then Captain Kitty said, "You realize I'll need to get Larson's permission for the wire. No sweat, though. I'm sure he'll go for it. He's wanted to bag Sands for years. Drop in later this afternoon and we'll talk some more about the timing."

As we headed for the door to her office, the Captain called out, "We might be moving you over to the Fourth in the next few days."

"Why, Captain?"

"That woman we found near the reservoir."

"The one with the wings?"

"That's it. Larson doesn't like freaky work like that. He wants to wrap it up quickly before the papers jump all over it. And so far, the boys we have on it haven't turned anything up."

"When do you want us on it?"

"Like, now. And Alex, I have a piece of good news for you. Remember Aramis Walker?"

"Of course. My favorite gangbanger."

"Aramis has decided to drop the brutality charge against you."

"Why?"

"Someone didn't like his table manners. He was shanked last night in the dining hall at Woonsocket. Six times. You got lucky, Detective Larch. Some of us thought Aramis might have had a case. Now watch your step out there. And if you feel the need to hit someone, start with your partner. That goes for you, too, Detective Martell."

Once outside, Alex and I were both in grin city. "This calls for a celebration," we said almost at the same time. "And we know where," I added as we headed to Martelli's, my family's restaurant on Federal Hill, for a long lunch and a couple of glasses of Amarone.

CHAPTER THREE

SANTINO VOLPE had done it again. On the counter in front of me were seven pale, rosebud-pink slices of veal scaloppini, cut almost razor thin across the grain: three for Linda and three for me, with one to spare. There was only one butcher in all of Providence who could provide veal this tender and knew how to slice it correctly, and that was Santino, whose shop was four doors down from my family's restaurant, now run by my uncle Sal. Veal piccata, which cooked in minutes, would be the centerpiece of the dinner I was preparing tonight. The opening act would be a seafood salad that had been on Martelli's menu since my grandfather opened the restaurant in 1937. The main ingredients—squid, shrimp, lobster, octopus, and crabmeat—came from a store next door to Santino's, Rigano's Fish and Seafood, whose motto was "Our fish are so fresh you almost want to slap them." God bless Federal Hill, Providence's Italian section, better than New York's Little Italy or Boston's North End.

I was feeling great. I had been on a high all day. Not only had Captain Kitty given us a go-ahead for our plan to nail Bernie Sands—"Larson's gung ho for it. I'm red-flagging this, guys. Get it together fast. Next week at the latest"—but, almost as good, Linda would be home for dinner tonight. We hadn't sat down for a meal in over a week, and I missed looking at her over the table, her sweet face lit softly by votive candles. An image of her the day we first met, eight years ago, hair plastered to her head from a sudden thunderstorm and still looking beautiful, came suddenly into focus.

My wife was indeed a beautiful woman. Smart and funny, too. So why the fuck had things been so shitty lately between the two of us? More fights than on the undercard at the Friday Night Fights in New Bedford, and a whole lot less sex. When we did get together, it was still great, but lately it was once a week at best. Linda worked for Dunwich Capital, the leading venture capital firm in town, and her crazy, relentless schedule meant that we ate most of our meals, *when* we ate them together, either ad hoc or on the run. Pizza one night, Chinese the next, all takeout, and all with the strong taste of the containers they came in. To me, this was a sacrilege. I come from a family that loves to eat. And to cook. We had spent, or rather Linda had spent, close to $60,000 on the kitchen—Gaggenau six-burner, Viking double-glass wall oven, Sub-Zero fridge, double Bulthaup sink, stainless steel cabinets and countertops, even a Bosch dishwasher—yet all we seemed to do in it was open containers of pork lo mein.

Tonight would be different. I went to the kitchen closet and pulled out my creamy-white chef's jacket. Stitched in blue script on the front pocket was my name, my real name, Danny Martelli. My father dropped the *i* when he opened his law office, two years before I was born. He always said that he did it to save money on the cost of the sign above the door. Though I've officially been Martell since I was born, I always think of myself as a Martelli. As my uncle Sal, who runs the family restaurant, says, "Martelli is a good, solid name with deep roots, like a big Barolo wine. Martell is the name of a so-so brandy."

Humming along with Ella—I kept a stack of her CDs in a corner of the counter—I began cooking the seafood over a low flame. A warm feeling of pleasure, almost like a trance, wrapped around me whenever I cooked. I had been doing it since I was a kid, and all the motions of the process, the stirring, the shaking of the salt, the drizzling of the olive oil, brought a comfort and relaxation that you get with a good massage.

The phone rang. It was my mother.

"Are we going to see you and Linda on Sunday?"

"Of course, Mom. We'll be there."

"Your brother has a new girlfriend. I think he's bringing her."

"I know. He told me about her yesterday. Nice Italian girl from Barrington. Just what you always wanted for him. Right, Mom?"

"What's wrong with an Italian girl, Mr. Detective?"

"Just kidding. How's Dad?"

"On the treadmill in the basement."

My father had had a mild heart attack a few years back and now exercised with the intensity of a high-wire performer.

"Tell him to give me a call."

"Daniel, the call should come from you. You know that."

Since the time I dropped out of law school to join the PD, almost eleven years ago, the relationship between my father and me had been cool enough to successfully counter global warming. Though Teddy, my kid brother, was now working in the firm, my father had always seen me, his older son and namesake, as his partner and eventual successor. I'll never forget the night I told him my decision. "Now let me get this straight: you're leaving BU Law to become a Providence cop. That's what you said, right?"

"That's it, Dad. I don't want to be a lawyer. It's just not for me."

"Are you out of your mind, Danny? Do you know what a cop makes, for Christ's sake? Do you think I sent you to Brown and then to law school so you could pound a fucking beat in Wayland Square?"

"It's what I want to do, Dad. It's as simple as that."

"Simple is right. But I'm not going to let you do this. You're throwing your life away."

"How are you going to stop me? I'm not a kid anymore, Dad."

I could never forget it because we had the same exchange again and again. After a while, maybe a year or two after Linda and I got married, we both settled into a relationship dominated by silence. Like that wall the Israelis built, there was something between us that didn't make sense but that neither of us could stop from being there.

I finished the seafood salad and decided to pause for a Stoli on the rocks, when Linda walked into the kitchen.

"How's my favorite detective chef?" she said, after circling my lips with her tongue. "Mmm, you taste good. Chopin?"

"Close but no cigar. Want me to pour you one?"

"I'd love it, but I have to get back to the office after dinner."

Go easy, Danny, I told myself. *You're going to start to shout, and that will lead nowhere. A little anger management is called for here. Let's keep the explosion small.*

"You're kidding, aren't you? I thought we'd have a nice, relaxed dinner tonight. Be together. If you want to eat on the run we could have met at fucking Burger King."

"Don't yell at me, honey. You don't know how difficult it was for me to get away at all. We're closing the Supino Industries buyout tonight. Everyone's working their asses off."

She's right. Finish cooking the damn dinner and make the best of it. There's always another night. Don't make this into a big thing. Aw, who the hell are you kidding?

"You know, Linda, why don't we just skip dinner tonight. I hate to see you miss any of the closing. After all, it's only a meal." She tried to get me to turn my back on the prick inside me, but I couldn't do it. A few tears later, and Linda was gone. My eye caught the slices of veal sitting in a line on a strip of wax paper, like planes waiting to take off. I picked one up, weighing it in my palm. Would it stick to the ceiling if I tossed it up hard? Maybe. Why not throw them all up? Let it rain down scaloppini when

Linda comes in at midnight or three in the morning in search of her yogurt. But I couldn't do that to this veal. To Linda? Maybe. To veal as beautiful as this? Never. And then I had an idea. Alex. Maybe he could come over for dinner. I called his cell, but as soon as I said, "Hey, man, how about…," I heard the sound of men shouting in the background. Damn it, I had forgotten that this was Alex's war-gaming night.

"Okay, I can hear that this is not a good time to talk," I said. "How about coming over to my place for dinner after you defeat the Germans or the Romans, or whoever the fuck you're fighting tonight?"

"I'm scheduled to dine elsewhere tonight. After this—and by the way, we're in the middle of the Battle of the Wilderness—I have a late date with a spinning instructor."

"A new target on your radar scope?"

"Very. I met her yesterday. She works at my gym."

"Sounds delightful."

"Time will tell. I can't judge her wit or her intellect, but she certainly must have endurance."

I sat there for a while before going to the freezer and pouring myself another nerve-numbing vodka, straight up. After draining the glass, I then set about joylessly preparing dinner.

CHAPTER FOUR

IT'S LATE *at night, and the man totes a large bundle over his shoulder, fireman-style, through a densely wooded area, the trees so tightly packed that to move forward he has to slide around them, like a skier on a slalom course. This is not a casual walker's terrain, and the man has good reason to believe that his solitude will not be interrupted. In fact, no one will see him. He's so familiar with this section that he has no trouble finding the one small clearing, even though the only light comes from a three-quarter moon shrouded in clouds. He's totally at ease, so much so that he's listening to Beethoven's* Missa Solemnis *through a headset attached to an iPod looped to his belt.*

He places his load on the ground and slowly stretches. He's carried it in from his truck, parked on the edge of the park a quarter-mile away. He loosens the sheet and stares down at a young woman. He kneels and searches his jacket pockets for something. He pulls out a badger brush and some powder. Holding a small flashlight between his teeth, he again dusts the woman's face, then moves toward her eyes, which are closed and puffy. He reapplies mascara, then, finally, adds a slash of bright red lipstick.

The man opens a small shoulder bag and pulls out two large swaths of fabric. He reaches down and attaches the material with pins to her shoulders.

He looks at her for a few moments. Woman? No. She's now an angel. He stands, tosses everything into the bag, and silently slips back into the woods ahead of him. Ghostlike.

CHAPTER FIVE

"**WHY THE** hell do we have to hump all the way up here to Federal Hill for a coffee every morning? There's a perfectly good Starbucks around the corner from the precinct house."

"Because, Poster Boy, as I've told you endless times, the espresso here is the real thing. Deep, dark, and mysterious. It's wop truth serum. Starbucks is McDonald's in a cup. I'm Italian, and I need real coffee." I knew why Alex was in a pissy mood. The reason was easy to divine. "How'd you do last night?"

"I already told you. We're still in the middle of the Battle of the Wilderness. We won't finish for at least a month."

"Shmuck, I meant the spinning instructor."

"Oh, that," said Alex as he slowly stirred his coffee. I had seen this many times before. Alex would never outright lie to me, but he was proud of his "lady-killer" reputation, and he was obviously scrambling on how to explain why it didn't work out.

"Yes, that."

"I guess you mean Whitney Rappaport. The spinner from hell."

"That bad, huh?"

"Worse. On the plus side, she has an ass that looks as hard as a wall in a jai alai fronton. Plus a rack you'd need pitons to climb. Those are the positives. But they're negated by a major flaw." Alex extracted the spoon from his cappuccino and slowly licked off the foam. "She's the quintessential commitment lady. Good old-fashioned freestyle humping does not fit into her plan. Certainly not on the first date. Nor probably on the second, third, or fourth. This gal has her sights on the long-term relationship that ends you know where. So that's my confession. I not only didn't score, but didn't even get into the on-deck circle."

The sky outside the coffeehouse was darkening to the color of a fresh bruise. It looked like the forecast of rain would be correct. I pulled out my list of to-dos from my inside jacket pocket. I'm a list maker. I've been doing it since I was a kid. While drinking my orange juice, I always write down what I have to do. The suspects, witnesses, snitches that Alex and I will see that day. The reports I have to write.

The name at the top of the list this morning was Lamar Purvis. Purvis, a heavy middle-aged African American, owned a rib joint on the north side. The week before there had been a drive-by shooting outside his place, and Alex and I were sure that he knew who the shooter was.

"What's our first stop?" asked Alex.

"I was thinking maybe Lamar."

"Why don't we pay him a visit around lunchtime? His ribs are supposed to be pretty good."

"Not a bad idea. But let's do takeout and tell him to meet us at the station later. I don't think we'll get much out of him in his joint. When did we say we'd meet Molly Juste?"

"Later this afternoon. We're supposed to call her at Al Forno's. She's a hostess there. Let me see that list." Alex looked at my list for a moment and then handed it back. "How about kicking our day off with Artie the Hat?"

Arthur Nardello, aka Artie the Hat, was a low-level mob guy who specialized in bust-outs. He'd rent an empty space on a busy street, always under someone else's name, set it up as an electronics or clothing store, and start to order inventory. He'd promptly pay the first bills that came in, and once his credit was established, he'd then order a ton of merchandise and vacate the store with all the goods before the next month's invoices even arrived.

"Good idea. He could be helpful on the Baldoria brothers piece of business. Where do we find him?"

"We don't have to gas up the car. He's three doors down. The wife owns a beauty parlor, and the Hat has his office in the back."

"You might not know a lot of things, Danny Boy, but you sure as shit know Federal Hill."

As we got up from the table, Alex's cell phone rang.

"Larch here. Yeah. No shit. Where? We'll be there in five minutes."

"What's up?"

"That was Kitty. They found another one. This time it's on our turf. Let's get going."

Norris Park was a pie-shaped wedge of green surrounded by row houses on three sides and dilapidated warehouses on the other. They all dated from the turn of the century, and they needed more than a coat of paint to look good again. Its nine acres included swings and teeter-totters, basketball and bocce courts, and, this being a city park, a few wooded, quiet places used to conduct the usual illicit sex acts and drug transactions.

The crime scene people were already there. Eddie Breslin, the department's photographer, was busy snapping away. The area had already been taped off, and the few people in the park were being kept a good two hundred feet away by a half dozen patrolmen.

"When do you think it happened?" I asked Captain Kitty when we got to the body.

"Last night. Though it probably didn't happen here."

The woman was young, no older than midtwenties. Unlike the first one, she was black, but the powder on her face gave her skin the color of wet cement. Like the one who had been found two weeks before in Kiser Park, on the other side of town, she was wrapped in a blue sheet. Under the body two loops of silk flared out.

"What the fuck is that?" asked Alex.

"Someone said they look like wings."

"She won't fly far with those," said Alex.

"Save the jokes for open-mike night, Larch. We've got a big problem here. We have to move fast. If the papers and TV find out about these 'touches,' they'll be all over us. This is the creepy kind of stuff they love. We have to keep a tight lid on this. Got it?"

"Yeah, Captain. Who's handling the other one?"

"Hughes and Miley."

"We'll get together with them as soon as we get back to the station," I said.

"See me first thing tomorrow morning. The ID on the first one turned up nine busts for soliciting. I wouldn't be surprised if this lady had been in the same business."

Captain Kitty turned and walked toward the park gate.

"I don't like this at all," I said.

CHAPTER SIX

I COULDN'T believe it, but Linda was standing outside her office building waiting for me. On time. A first. Well, maybe a second. Usually when I pick her up there, I bring at least two magazines, sometimes a book. It's not that she's a disorganized person who's always running late. She's as organized as an air traffic controller. It's just that she's not in the business where when the clock hits five you turn off the light and head home. I understand that, but it still bothers me. And though I don't talk to anyone about it, the money she makes annoys me even more. *Pisses me off* would be a better way of putting it. Sure, I like all the things the money brings us: my car (the BMW was a Christmas present last year), our house (with a Narragansett beach house in the planning stage), and vacations (when she can get away!). Sure, I realize that if she worked as a teacher or something like that, our two salaries together would give us a much different lifestyle. Like a small house in a so-so neighborhood, and the only beach house we'd be considering would be a two-week rental in August.

"My husband looks very thoughtful tonight," she said when she got into the car.

"Would you believe I was thinking of you?" I answered as I leaned over for a kiss.

"I believe everything you tell me."

"Maybe that's because I don't tell you that much."

"How about another kiss, and then tell me when we're having dinner."

I pulled her over and gave her a real kiss. Then she took over. Linda could do a lot of things well, but her kissing was outstanding. It was sort of like those water slides for kids—long and wet and I never knew when or where it would end.

"That was very nice."

"You always say that." Linda pulled down the visor and put on some more lipstick.

"That's because I'm an appreciative guy. Maybe later you'll give me something else to appreciate."

"I think we might be able to arrange that. Now, where are we having dinner? I'm famished."

"Giorgio's," I said with a huge smile. It was a real coup.

"Giorgio's!" she squealed like a rock-concert fan. "You're a genius. On a Friday night? How'd you do it?"

"I'll tell you later."

I hadn't seen so much excitement from her in a long while, and it was very satisfying. Who doesn't like being called a genius, so I decided not to let her know it was just dumb luck. I'd embroider the story until it was a testimony to my smartness. Truth was, I had called the restaurant, the hottest in town, seconds after someone had canceled. I had discovered this by pleading my case to the woman on reservations, who surprised me—and probably herself—by offering me the space. Sometimes funny things happen.

"By the way," I said, "we're meeting Alex and his date there."

"Oh, great," said Linda, in what she likely thought was a neutral voice.

I knew she wasn't pleased but had reined herself in, not her usual style. Her attitude toward Alex was mixed, somewhere in no-man's-land between lukewarm and dislike. She was outspoken about almost everything and accustomed to getting her way, like a spoiled child. Tonight she was, for her, on good behavior, though I didn't know why.

"Come on," I said. "We'll have fun."

"I bet."

"Oh, stop it, will you? Alex is my best friend."

That put a halt to all conversation, like a splash of icy water. We rode in silence all the way to the restaurant.

There, at Giorgio's best table, center stage, was Alex, smiling like he had won the lottery. Next to him was a pretty, slender brunette with a whiff of Julia Roberts about her—big mouth, big smile. Alex bounded up and kissed Linda on both cheeks. Very continental. It didn't take much sleuthing to discover that Karen was a stewardess (excuse me, a flight attendant) for JetBlue and wasn't the slightest bit intimidated by the handsome blond detective next to her. We chatted about the virtues of the airline—offering no airline food, just snacks, being high on the list—then went on to order. We wanted to catch a movie afterward, so we didn't linger. Alex and I are suckers for a Bruce Willis film.

Midway through our appetizers, Karen, eager as a teenager, broached the subject you could see she had been dying to raise.

"Alex," she said, with her big smile, "I saw in the paper yesterday that another woman was found murdered in the park. What happened?"

"Just what you think, my pet," said Alex. "Nothing special. Probably a boyfriend who went into a rage because the gal gave him only a small piece of her terrine."

"Come on. What's the real story?" said Karen, disappointed.

"That's not enough for you? Crimes of passion involving a terrine are quite common."

"We'll get the guy real soon," I told her. "Then we can all read about it in the newspapers."

"Don't forget TV," added Alex.

When the check came, Linda opened her purse and started to pull out her American Express card. Platinum, of course. She caught a look from me and put it away. I might make a fraction of what she makes, but I'd be damned if I'd let her pick up the check. We had been through this before, but every once in a while she slipped.

"Never forget," I told her the first time, "I'm your husband, not a client. I pay. Always."

After Alex and I settled the bill (both of us have green AmEx cards, by the way), we headed outside to the cars. The multiplex was about twenty minutes away, and I decided to follow him.

The lights of the restaurant were still in my rearview mirror when Linda put her hand on my leg. "Let's skip the movie," she said in a low voice. "I want to be alone with you." I took my eyes off the road for a few seconds and searched her face. What I saw in her expression gave me a very intense and pleasant jolt. "Use your cell. Tell him anything, but just get us home."

When we were at our place, Linda ran upstairs, and I went to the kitchen to get a couple of beers. My hand was on the refrigerator door when I thought how stupid I was. Sure, I was thirsty, but it wasn't for beer. What I wanted was upstairs. I raced up to the bedroom. Linda had already stripped her clothes off and was lying facedown on the bed.

"Linda," I said, almost choking on her name, as I moved to the bed, pulling off my pants and shirt on the way. I turned her over and pulled her into my arms.

"I've been thinking about this all night," she said. "Couldn't you feel it?"

"I've got to work on my mind-reading skills," I barely got out.

We began to kiss. Our hands moved down over our bodies, and we made love slowly, very slowly. I don't know how long we were at it, but we both knew without saying it that it was one of the best times we'd had in months. I held her tightly and almost immediately fell asleep, thinking, then dreaming, that maybe our problems were over.

Sometimes in the middle of the night I sat up with a jolt of confusion. It took me a few seconds to get my bearings. Yes, I was in bed. And yes, Linda was sleeping next to me, curled around herself, her hair splayed out around her head like a lace collar. I felt a rise of desire, but I stopped. This was where we had left off last night. I had been convinced that all our anger, disappointments, disconnects were over, and all it had taken was one spectacular bout of sex.

But who was I fooling? I knew it wasn't that easy. I lay back in bed, thinking, as if I had hit the jackpot, that the only real solution now or later was to go to sleep. But I couldn't. Five minutes later I got up and took half an Ambien. It worked.

CHAPTER SEVEN

MOLLY JUSTE lay sprawled on the floor. Her gray eyes were fixed, and her skin was pale as sand. Blood trickled down from the crook of her left arm. A syringe was on the floor next to her. She was thirty-one but looked five years younger.

"You're a very attractive corpse, Ms. Juste," said Alex as he snapped away with a digital camera.

"Thank you, Detective Larch," she answered, talking through her teeth and not moving a muscle. Molly wanted to be an actress, and though I had no idea if she had the talent to make it, she sure as hell could play a murder victim.

Molly Juste was the centerpiece of our plan to put away Bernie Sands. The photos that Alex was taking would be given to the Flea, who would in turn hand them to Sands as proof that he had murdered Molly. Sands would then pay the Flea, the transaction recorded via the wire he would be wearing and also on video from a hidden camera, and Sands would be toast. Alex and I had tabled all our other cases (except Bernie Sand's) to work on what we were calling the Angel Murders.

"You sure this fake blood doesn't stain?" Molly asked.

"We got it in a store that sells Halloween stuff," I told her. "They swear it doesn't."

"Well, if it does, expect a dry-cleaning bill."

We had met with Molly the day before to set things up. The Flea was due to return from his pizza-eating contest in Scranton on Monday, and we finalized his part in the scheme by phone. Molly worked as a hostess at Al Forno's, a great restaurant near the river that took no reservations and where customers waited up to a couple of hours for a table. It was early, and the restaurant was reasonably quiet, so we ducked out behind the place, where we could talk.

"You sure you want to go through with this?" I asked.

"I'll do anything to help put this creep away. Anyway, I don't have any other, better roles coming my way, so I'm delighted to do it."

"Looks like you got a good gig here," said Alex.

"If you mean tips, you're right. It sure as hell beats some of my other jobs: supermarket checkout clerk, dog walker, guide on a sightseeing bus—and those are the good ones. You name it and I've done it."

You couldn't help but like Molly Juste. Her face, an almost perfect oval, was always in motion, and she smiled like she meant it. I don't know if she worked out, but her figure made you think she did. Though we already had her home phone number, Alex made a point of getting her number at the restaurant. I could see where this was going.

"Hey, Danny, why don't we make it look like the spike is in her arm?"

"How?"

"Like, Scotch-taping it. Here." He tossed me a roll, and I taped it to her forearm. "Pull the sleeve down a bit. Yes. That's perfect," he said, clicking away. "Ms. Juste, you look frighteningly believable. Look at these, Danny." He handed me the camera, and I started to scroll through the shots. "I might not be Cartier-Bresson, but you've got to admit they're pretty good."

"You're right, my man," I said. "You definitely have the makings of another career. Pretty soon you'll be doing passport photos."

"Let me give my favorite corpse a helping hand," said Alex as he helped Molly to her feet.

"My first starring role," she said, laughing. "But I don't think I'll put it on my résumé."

With a quick "Bye, guys," she opened the door to the hallway and began the long trek down the stairs. We were on the top floor of a warehouse that Captain Kitty had secured for our photo session, high enough for us to still hear Molly's footsteps clatter on the iron staircase.

Alex rushed to the door and threw it open.

"Hey, where do you think you're going?"

"I want to get her number at work."

"Dummy, you got it yesterday." Alex hit his forehead, signaling that he remembered the Post-it that was probably still jammed into his jacket pocket.

CHAPTER EIGHT

EVER SINCE I was a little kid, my family had lunch together every Sunday. Where? At Martelli's, of course. My uncle Sal was the titular host, together with my grandmother, who still lives in the apartment upstairs. That's where my father, his brother, and their three younger sisters were raised. Most of the time we numbered a dozen or so, but once in a while that number would double when a couple of my aunts and their families would make the trek to Providence from New Jersey, where they live. My other aunt, Teresa, lives in Santa Fe and shows up only at Christmas, and that's every other year at best. Since New Mexico is not known for its prosciutto and ricotta, Sal FedExes care packages to her on a monthly basis. Today was special since my kid brother was bringing his new girlfriend, Val. He had never done this before. I could see the family liked her. She was a big girl with a bigger smile, but best of all, she was Italian. She was quickly bookended at the table between my mother and grandmother. Within minutes, the three were laughing, and Val was receiving advice on everything from how to stuff a quail to the best place in town to have your hair streaked.

I sat between my aunt Minnie, Sal's wife, and Ric, their son. Ric's an insurance adjuster, and most of the time we talk about either the Red Sox or the Pats. There was a Pats game on (they were playing Miami), and we would periodically get up from the table and catch a few minutes of the action on the TV at the bar. I wasn't seated with my wife because, as usual, Linda was working. Due diligence on another big deal. Linda, who genuinely liked my folks, didn't care much for the Martelli-Martell lunch: "Too loud and too much food. And heaven help me if I leave something on my plate." Linda's a WASP, and right from the beginning I could see that heaps of food and conversations that were generally conducted at a decibel level people use when on opposite sides of a street were not for her. Occasionally I invited Alex, who's kind of an extended family member, but he'd begged off because he was going to the Cape to visit his sister.

Luckily Jimmy Warden was free. We talk all the time, but I hadn't seen him in almost a month. He sat opposite me, his massive forearms resting on the table like a large piece of furniture. Jimmy had eyes the color of granite, and though he had recently hit sixty-four, his hair was still mud brown and thick as a brush. He worked out daily, and his chest gave proof of that, bulging under the turtleneck he had on. I had met him my first day out of the Academy, and he, more than anyone else, had taught me what the police game was all about. I rode in the car with him for almost two years before he retired. Jimmy left because Bonnie, his wife, developed liver cancer, and he nursed her through the long downhill path that had ended the year before. He was both a friend and almost a father to me, coming into my life just after my own father sent me to Coventry for joining the force.

My father took up his regular position at the table—as far away from me as possible. Like negotiators at a high-level talk between two Koreas, we exchanged polite greetings before and after the meal.

This Sunday the meal consisted of sautéed scallops, roasted peppers with pignoli and golden raisins, headcheese, tiny meatballs in *arrabiata* sauce, and a salad of wild chicory with anchovy dressing. And that was just the first course. This was followed by fish (*branzino*), pasta (linguine with cockles), and meat (Florentine steak topped with crushed tomatoes and arugula).

The red wine was a great Barolo, and the white, dry as tinder, was from Sicily. I left before dessert (yes, there's always dessert), and after the kisses and the hugs, I decided to stop at Linda's office. Who knows, maybe she'd worked enough for the day and wanted to spend some time with me.

Her firm had an entire floor in a new office building downtown. You could tell by the furnishings, the art, and the view that Dunwich Capital was minting money. On a clear day, you got the feeling you could see as far as Boston. When I got up there, it looked like a normal weekday, lots of people staring at computer screens, all the glass-enclosed offices occupied. Except for Linda's.

"She left a couple of hours ago, Mr. Martell," Traci, the receptionist, told me.

"Did she say where she was going?"

"Not to me."

"When do you think she'll be back?"

"I have no idea. Want me to have her call you when she gets back?"

When I got downstairs, there was a parking ticket under the wiper. Shit. I had forgotten to put my police ID on the dashboard. I'd pay the damn thing because it wasn't worth the hassle to have the ticket pulled. As I drove home, I remembered a nasty line my father hit me with after I graduated from the Academy: "You really got it knocked now, Danny. Imagine, you can always park in front of a hydrant and never get a ticket. Isn't that terrific?"

I called out for Linda when I walked into our house, but she wasn't there. I went upstairs and changed into sweats and headed for the basement to work out. Linda had set up a first-class gym down there the year before. Treadmill, stair climber, stationary bike, Cybex weight center, heavy and speed bags. Got the picture? She even put in a sauna, which we used a lot at first but now functioned as a place to store some lawn furniture. I turned on the Pats game and got on the treadmill. I set the incline and pace above my usual levels to work off some of the meal. I always felt like Dom DeLuise afterward, and today was no exception. I was bathed in sweat after a half hour but kept it up for another fifteen minutes. After drying off, I did some serious reps with free weights and then three sets of abdominals. I was halfway through my stretching routine when I heard Linda.

"Down here, baby!" I called out.

"This place really smells like a gym," she said, bending down to kiss me as I finished stretching my quads.

"Do you know I came to the office to free you from the bonds of due diligence?"

"I got the message."

"Where were you?"

"Movie."

"What'd you see?"

"A French film."

"Good?"

"Just okay. I had to get away from the place. Sometimes the pressure just gets to me. How was lunch?"

"Great. And, as usual, massive. That's why I've been exercising my ass off."

"Poor baby."

I got up and put my arms around her. "I've got an idea. A dirty one."

"That sounds interesting. Where does this idea take place?"

"In the sauna. Just give me a moment to get out the lawn chairs and then fire it up. Won't take but a minute."

It wasn't long before we were both as slick as seals, our skin as wet as our mouths. We coiled around each other on the slatted bench. I sat Linda up and started to put her legs over my shoulders.

"I'm not in the mood for that, baby."

"I've never heard that from you before."

"Let me do you instead."

"I'm not going to argue with an offer like that."

Later, we barely made it up the stairs to our bedroom. When I clawed to the surface from a nap that was as deep as a coma, Linda was gone, replaced by a note: *Dear: Had to go back to the factory. Hope to see you for dinner. By the way, you have the best ideas. Love, L.*

CHAPTER NINE

EVERY CITY has places where you can find sex. We're not a big city, but we don't take a backseat to the better-known metropolises, where you can get anything you're looking for. Monday morning Alex and I decided to methodically check these areas after the second victim turned out to have several solicitation busts on her rap sheet.

Her name was Dani Robson, but, like the first victim, she had worked under several other names: Dawn Hummock, Alyce Packer, and Shar King. Neither of us has ever spent time in vice, but we had met a number of the "ladies" while investigating other cases, and one in particular had always proven to be a reliable source. Her name was LaVelle Stubbins, and we usually could find her on a corner a few blocks from the Biltmore. We didn't have to wait more than fifteen minutes before we saw LaVelle walk down the street. She had a passion for wigs (Madonna, Cher, Supremes, you name it), and today she was into Liza.

"How 'bout a cup of coffee, LaVelle?" I asked as we got out of the car.

"If it isn't my two favorite civil servants. How you doing this fine day, Detectives?"

"Not bad, LaVelle. Where you want to go?" asked Alex.

"There's a pretty good place around the corner. The Supreme Bean. Good latte and even better bagels. You'll spring for a bagel, too, I hope?"

The coffee shop was quiet, and we took a table in the back, away from the few people who were there.

"You recognize either of these two girls?" I slid the photos across to LaVelle.

She looked at the prints closely.

"These two ladies need major help in the makeup department. They're dead, right?"

"Very," Alex said.

"This one," she said, pointing to Dani Robson, "I've seen her around. Both on the street and at Trinity."

"The outreach program?"

She nodded, continuing to stir her coffee. She held the other photo up to the light.

"This one, I've never seen. Sure of it."

"The other one was named Dani."

"There's a lot of names on the street. And a lot of new girls. I just know I've seen her around."

"Ever talk to her?" I asked.

"Once. At Trinity."

"Remember anything of that?"

"She wanted to get visiting rights to see her kid. She was crying. Seemed like a long shot to me."

"Do you remember seeing her with any johns?"

"I keep my eye on my own business."

"What were you doing at the church, LaVelle?" asked Alex.

"They're helping me put together a business plan."

"Business plan?"

"Not for my pussy work," she said, laughing. "I'm going to open a coffeehouse someday soon. Not here. In Boston. I got most of the money put away. I've known for a long time that my ass can only take me so far."

"Why a coffeehouse?"

"It's harder than shit to smoke inside these days, but you can still drink coffee. And like crack, it's addictive. I've looked at a lot of franchises, you know, Subway, things like that, but coffee feels right. I even got my name picked out. I'm gonna call it Starfucks, but with a little star in place of the *f*. People won't forget that."

CHAPTER TEN

THE EPISCOPAL Church of the Holy Trinity was a huge limestone pile that was once located in the midst of a solid middle-class neighborhood. Over the years, like a glacier melting, the congregants slowly moved out and poverty and crime moved in. The church was headed by Father Michael Coles, who was known to all in Providence as Militant Mike. He was constantly in the paper or on radio and TV, promoting one cause or another, whether it was heading up a rent strike or leading a march on city hall for the homeless.

"Could we see Father Coles, please?" I asked an older woman who sat behind a computer in the rectory office. She had a huge mound of spun-sugar hair that was bluer than the tie I used to wear for assembly in grade school.

"He's not here," she said without looking up.

"Do you know when he'll be back?" Alex asked.

"When he finishes dishing out lunch." She looked at her watch. "In a half hour or so."

"We'll wait," I said.

"If you go to the basement next door, you can see him now. You can even get something to eat. We're serving gazpacho and meatloaf today."

We walked next door, where a bedraggled line of people snaked down the block. Inside we immediately spotted Father Coles. He was wearing a chef's toque and an apron that read, in a florid script, Holy Trinity Café. Along with four other helpers, he was in the middle of the serving line, dishing out mounds of mashed potatoes as the people slowly passed. We had met him a year before when there had been a break-in and a large silver crucifix had been stolen. We had recovered the cross the following week on a tip attached to a fence on Federal Hill. Two kids had swiped it, and after the recovery, Father Coles didn't want to press charges.

"I'll be with you boys in a minute. Why don't you wait in the kitchen."

Ten minutes later he walked in. After taking off his apron, he shook our hands. He was a big man. I had read that he played tackle at Williams, and, though now in his late sixties, he still looked like he could take care of himself. His silver-gray hair was cut marine boot camp short, and his blue eyes shined as if they were backlit. We followed him into an adjoining room that was lined floor to ceiling with pine shelves that held cans of food.

"What can I do for you boys?" he asked after he closed the door. "Some of those we help might get a little spooked if they knew two of Providence's finest were on the premises, so it's best we talk here."

"Thanks for seeing us so quickly, Father," said Alex.

"We understand you run an outreach program here for prostitutes."

"You're Danny, right? And you're…It's not Alan…no…Alex. That's it. Alex."

"Good memory, Father."

"What can you tell us about the program, Father?" I asked again.

"We started it about two years ago. I'd say it's quite a success. We offer a wide range of assistance to women who want to get off the street. Psychological, medical, nutrition, child care, drug and alcohol counseling, and career training. In fact, any problem they may have or avenue they might want to follow. Our doors are open Monday through Friday from six to midnight. We see over forty women a week."

"Would you take a look at these, Father?" said Alex as he handed over photos of the dead women.

He looked at each one carefully. "They're…"

"Yes. Dead. They were murdered. They both had numerous arrests for soliciting. That's why we're here."

"They don't look familiar to me. You see, our program is staffed by a great group of volunteers. They work closely with the women. They're the ones you should see. If you go to my office, Miss Martin will give you a list of their names. Each one comes here at least twice a week. You'll have to come back a couple of times to see them all."

"Thanks, Father. We'll try to get back here tomorrow or the next day," I said.

"So very sad," he said softly to himself as he looked at the photos again. "How did they die?"

"They were both strangled," I told him.

"Such a hard life. And then this. A dark, terrible ending. Did they have family?"

"We're working on that now."

"Do you remember the boys who took the cross?" he said, handing the photos back. We both nodded. "They're in our basketball program and come to services regularly. So, you see, there's hope for all of us."

CHAPTER ELEVEN

"EDDIE," I said to the Flea, "you're a positive fashion plate."

"What do you mean, Detective?"

"The cornrows, man. Have you switched from competitive eating to rapping? You look like a brother."

"You like them?" said the Flea, running his hand over the tight rows. "My girlfriend did them for me this weekend. She's African American. It was good luck for the pizza-eating contest. I came in third. She's gonna do them once a week now. Aren't they a bitch?"

"How's the competitive eating going, Flea?" Alex asked.

"Great. I just broke into the IFOCE's top one hundred. I'm going against Cookie Jarvis next month in Akron. He's ranked number three. He holds a bunch of records. That competition is in cannolis. Cookie's record is twenty-four in six minutes. I'm shooting for at least sixteen. That would put me in the money."

"Now sit still, and let Sy do his job," I said.

Alex and I and our tech guy, Sy Harris, were crammed with the Flea into one of the small rooms that ranged along a hall off Captain Kitty's office. The rooms were all equipped with a desk, two chairs, and a two-way mirror. A fat man with a wire taped to his chest might have piqued the interest of someone who came upon the correct window, but the Captain kept tight control of the space around her. I knew there was no one else on the floor.

As soon as the job was done, we commandeered one of the vans from the garage, a dirty, mud-splattered number that gave no hint of what was inside. The diner where the Flea was to meet Bernie Sands was located on Sabin Street next to the convention center. Alex, Sy, and another techie stayed in the van, one on the recorder, the other with a video camera trained on a booth by the window. Alex had stopped by the diner earlier and arranged to keep the space unoccupied until we finished with the operation.

I went into the diner first and took a booth near the door. I ordered some eggs and coffee. Ten minutes later, right on plan, the Flea walked in. I didn't have to wait long before Bernie Sands arrived. I kept my head down in my newspaper. He was a big man who had never been in good shape. His face shined as if he had just stepped out of a greenhouse, and he carried a large, battered black briefcase. He was in his early forties but looked at least ten years older. If they had a picture next to the definition of *slumlord* in the dictionary, Sands's face would be perfect.

Sands sat down with the Flea and immediately got to the point. Their voices were low but not low enough. The wire was working perfectly. Through my earpiece I heard every word.

"Well, did you get it done?" asked Sands.

"Don't I even get a 'Hello, Eddie'? Maybe a 'How you been? You're looking good'? You know I dropped another fifteen pounds since the last time I saw you."

"Yeah, you look like Brad Pitt. Now answer my question. Have you gotten rid of my problem?"

"Yes. Last night. Now let me see the money."

"Show me some proof. Then we can talk money."

The Flea pulled the Polaroids of Molly Juste from his jacket and spread them like a deck of cards in front of Sands. He studied them closely and then looked over at the Flea and smiled. I was surprised he knew how to do that.

"She never looked better. It's great to be rid of that miserable bitch," he said, pushing a large envelope across to the Flea.

"Fifteen thousand. Nothing bigger than fifties. Just don't count it here."

Then the Flea belched loudly, which he could do on command, signaling that the money had been passed. That was my cue, and I rose immediately, went to the booth, and cuffed Sands.

"You motherfucker!" Sands screamed at the Flea, who had slid out of the booth. "Don't think you can get away with this. I've got people who can take care of you, you rotten piece of shit."

Alex came into the diner and read Sands his rights. We pushed him toward the door. Then Alex, feeling frisky, tripped him. He fell with a groan to the floor.

"Sorry, Bernie. I'm such a klutz." Alex kicked him in his side, triggering more groans, and then hauled him up. We ushered him into the van to take him to the station for booking.

Sands, his face red, tried to get in the last word as I closed the back door.

"You're dead!" he yelled at the Flea, who was standing at the doorway to the diner.

"Better watch what you say, Bernie. You got enough on your plate already!" the Flea shouted back, laughing.

CHAPTER TWELVE

THERE WERE four volunteers at the outreach center when we got there the next night. They were seated in a couple of pews near the front. They were the only people there, and our footsteps made a hollow drumbeat as we walked up the aisle. They all stood as we neared them. After quick introductions, the youngest and prettiest, Tanya Bohlen, pulled a thermos of coffee from her bag and poured us each a cup.

"Hey, this is great," said Alex, smiling at Tanya, who we later found out owned a florist shop near the Brown campus and had made the coffee. It was good and strong, and this, coupled with the fact that she had a great body, led him to assume his favorite opening role: Mr. Compliment.

"This is the best coffee I think I've ever tasted."

Subtlety, you see, was not part of his chasing repertoire.

"I got the coffee at Zabar's last week when I was in New York for the orchid show," she said, smiling back at him. "Vienna Roast."

"Obviously you have a talent for making the right choices," he said, and then, if you can believe it, winked at her.

As soon as everyone was seated again, we took down names, phone numbers, occupations—the usual. Ellen Sprague taught Spanish in a high school near the airport. She was in her sixties but had the energy of someone twenty years younger. I wouldn't have been surprised if she'd Rollerbladed her way to the church. The third was Brooks Shelby, an art conservator, who worked at the museum at Rhode Island School of Design and specialized in the paintings of the early Renaissance. He looked the part of a conservator: tall, thin, dapper, and tweedy, complete with a bow tie and a pipe (unlit, of course). The fourth was Arnie Lanoff, a tall, muscular guy who owned a used-car lot near our precinct. All four were members of the church and had been involved with the program since its inception. I wondered what brought them to it. Perhaps Father Coles? Or were they simply garden-variety do-gooders?

Ellen Sprague's reason for being there needed no explanation. The school where she taught was in a low-income area, and she was constantly worried about her girls. The steps from flirtation to trading favors for drugs inevitably led to prostitution.

After the volunteers explained what they did there—job counseling, safe-sex instruction, help with child care and housing—we showed them the two photos. Ellen, Brooks, and Arnie said they had never seen either woman before, but Tanya said one looked familiar.

"But we get quite a few who just come in once," she added.

"Tell you what," I said. "We'll leave these with you. Pass them around to the others. If anyone remembers either one, call us right away."

"Anytime," said Alex, writing his phone number on his card before handing it to Tanya. "Thanks for your help," he added.

As we were leaving, Alex pulled Brooks Shelby aside. He had read that the museum had a show of naval and army battles from the eighteenth and nineteenth centuries. "I fight some battles, but in miniature. War gaming."

"Why don't you come by?" said Brooks with a smile. "I'd be happy to give you a tour. But don't wait too long. The show's only up for another two weeks."

CHAPTER THIRTEEN

PROVIDENCE HAS a lot of good restaurants, but I've never had a good meal with Captain Kitty. You see, our Captain is a vegetarian. Militant variety. For a short while, she even toyed with becoming a vegan. Scary. So that's why we wound up the next day having lunch with her at a new place a couple of blocks from the station, the Green Palate. You guessed it: a vegetarian restaurant. I couldn't even get a Coke in the place. Alex settled for an avocado-and-sprout wrap, while I went for a salad of seasonal greens with (I crossed my fingers) Italian dressing. Mistake. The dressing was the color of mud and tasted like cough medicine.

"I got a call from Grisham this morning," said Kitty.

"The guy who wrote *The Firm*?" asked Alex.

"He wishes. This was Murray Grisham. From the *Journal.*"

"Uh-oh," I mumbled.

"That's what I thought, Danny. And I was right. Someone's talking. He knows about the wings. Also the makeup."

"Shit."

"We have to move fast on this. He doesn't have enough yet for a big story, but I don't think he's far off. Can you imagine how TV will play this thing? I can feel the heat already. Please tell me you've got something."

We ran her through what we'd dug up so far. Not much.

"We want to set up surveillance on Westminster and one on India," Alex told her.

"That's where they worked. He's not finding his victims at Barnes and Noble," I added.

"We'll run the plates on every car that even slows down to look at the action."

"That makes sense, but what if he's corralling them somewhere else?"

"Such as?"

"Bars…where they live…I don't know."

"Captain, I think right now the street is our best bet," I said.

"I hope you're right."

"We're meeting with Hughes and Miley later to see if they've turned up anything," Alex added.

"I spoke to them this morning. Nada."

We ate in silence for a while. I moved my salad around a bit. "I got a call on Sands. He'll make bail this afternoon. Three hundred K, and they're pulling his passport. There's no way he's going to beat this one. Serious time for a serious creep."

"Amen," Alex said.

"You have to agree that the Flea's delivered. How does it look for him?" I asked.

"The DA has what I would call an erectile condition regarding Mr. Mott. We're working on him, but there's no way he's going to walk. I'd say six months and he does four. That's the best they'll do."

"Well," Alex said, "I guess the Flea's going to miss the Nathan's hot dog competition this year."

CHAPTER FOURTEEN

THE NEXT night I got home at nine thirty, even later than the night before. I had worked alone all day, talking to park employees (there were seven) and residents of the houses that bordered the park. Nothing. Alex had been out in Woonsocket, where the mother of the last victim lived. Also nothing. We were scheduled to work together the next day. I tossed my keys on the hall table and called out for Linda. A third nothing.

I went into the kitchen to check the answering machine. Five messages: my mother ("Don't forget your grandmother's birthday"); my brother ("I got an extra ticket for the Sox tomorrow"); Linda's friend Sasha, calling for her ("Still thinking about what you told me. We have to talk"); Artie, the gardener ("I've got prices on the dwarf plum trees"); and my father ("Are we still on for lunch?"). That message, of course, was for Linda. I couldn't remember the last time I had had lunch alone with my father, but he and Linda lunched at least once a month. He thought my marrying Linda was the one smart move I had made in life since I'd gotten into Brown. He loved that she made ten times what I did. And though the only deal he ever made was to sell a couple of Laundromats my mother inherited when her father died, he was fascinated by all the transactions Linda was involved in. Whenever she showed up at the Sunday family lunches, he always sat next to her, and I could always hear him ask her questions about mezzanine financing, junk bonds, and subordinated debt. He was becoming an investment banker by proxy.

I went into the kitchen and grabbed a beer. Linda had told me when she left that morning that she wouldn't be too late and maybe she'd even cook us supper. Fat fucking chance. I finished the beer and opened another. She had closed a big deal the week before and saw a couple of weeks of early nights ahead. Another fat fucking chance. I called her at the office. Got her voice mail. Didn't leave a message. I switched to Stoli. The first one tasted so good that I had another. At eleven I ordered a pizza. With sausage and onions. Then I tried her cell. This time I left a message: "I'd like to say hi, but I'm too fucking mad. Where the hell are you? It would have been nice if you'd called to tell me when you were getting home. I guess that isn't a big enough deal for you."

I had one slice and half a bottle of red to go when she walked in.

"Hi," she said. I looked at the kitchen clock: 12:07. "Mind if I have a glass?" I kept my head down and took another bite. "I guess I'll be going to bed, since you have no interest in talking to me."

"Where the fuck have you been?" I said without looking up.

"I was out with Sasha. We had dinner."

"And dessert, too, I guess. It's after midnight on a Friday night. Why didn't you call?"

"I guess I forgot."

"What kind of fucking answer is that?"

"Sasha's having a problem at home. I was trying to help her. I didn't think calling you was that important. I'm sorry."

"Sorry's not enough. Fuck Sasha. You're supposed to think about me. We're supposed to be married."

"I can't talk to you when you're like this," she said, putting down her glass. "I'll see you in the morning."

I waited for her to go upstairs to our bedroom and close the door before I swept my arm across the table, knocking everything, including the wineglasses, to the floor. I went to the fridge for another Stoli, but the cracking of the glass shards under my shoes made me stop.

You've had enough, Danny. Another see-through and you'll do something that'll make you kick yourself in the ass tomorrow.

What do you think I might do?

You're thinking of going up there and throwing her ass out of bed.

You're a mind reader. What would I do after that?

You tell me.

I might put my tongue inside her.

So you're horny now?

No. I couldn't raise one if I tried.

So what are you doing?

I want to taste her.

Why?

You know why.

Tell me.

I can't.

Don't be a punk. Say it.

Okay. I want to see if she's been fucking someone else.

That's enough for tonight. You can go to bed now.

Thanks.

By the way...

What now?

Sleep in the guest room. It'll make things easier in the morning. And try to clean up this mess. You don't want Linda to cut her foot in the morning. Or do you?

CHAPTER FIFTEEN

I PULLED myself up from the guest room bed and zombie-walked into the bathroom to shave and shower. It was more than just a good habit. I have dark hair and a heavy beard, and if I skipped my morning ritual, I'd look like a Bowery bum by lunchtime. I had read somewhere that the Bowery no longer existed, that it had been turned into glass-enclosed office buildings for Verizon and the like, and condos for yuppies, but the way I felt, the old Bowery suited me best.

As I plowed my razor in a daze through the foam on my face, like a cross-country skier pushing mindlessly through deep snow, I could think about nothing but Linda. I put the razor down—it was just luck that I hadn't slashed myself—and, my heart pounding, walked over to our bedroom. I had been avoiding it, but I couldn't do that any longer. Everything was as I had left it. The bedspread, the sheets, nothing had been disturbed. No one, least of all Linda, had slept there.

By the time I reached the station, my anger was at full boil. The first person I met was Alex.

"What the fuck is wrong with you?" he asked, picking up on my mood immediately.

"None of your business."

"Oh, that's great. Thanks a lot."

"While you were out in Woonsocket, for all I know hitting on the vic's mother, I was here all day, pounding the fucking street. It's called working."

"Jesus. What bit your ass this morning?"

As soon as Alex left the office to get a coffee, I closed the door behind him and called Linda.

"I have to see you tonight. After work," I said.

"I don't know when I'll get out. My bosses are like hungry dogs. Whenever we finish a deal, they dig up another."

"What's that got to do with us?"

"Nothing. It was just a figure of speech for how this place operates. Now that there's a new deal on the table, it's full-court-press for everyone."

"Don't these pigs realize you have a life, too?" The question hung in the air. Finally I broke the silence. "We have to talk, Linda."

She did not answer me immediately. After a while, she said, "I don't think I'm ready for that yet."

"You're not 'ready.' What kind of answer is that?" When I heard myself shouting at her, I caught my breath and slowed down. But only for a moment.

"It's an honest answer."

"Oh, right. You're the honest one. You make me laugh. You always find an excuse for whatever you say or do." My voice was rising again.

"That's not true."

"True? I'll tell you what's true. If we go on like this, there'll be a day—maybe soon—when we see each other on the street but barely recognize the other person. Is that why we got married? Is this what you want?"

It took me a few seconds to hear the silence on the other end of the line, as final as the sun sinking on the horizon. Linda had hung up on me.

As soon as I could get away with it, without a word to Alex or anyone else, I left the station and drove over to Linda's office. It was near lunchtime, and as people poured out of the entrance,

I searched the crowd for Linda. I spent a half hour trying to read the paper but finally gave up and went into her office. The receptionist, a pretty young redhead, saw me coming and, before I reached her desk, pulled out an envelope and handed it to me, smiling.

"Thanks," I mumbled.

Back in the car, I ripped it open: *Danny*, it read, *I've left for the day. Won't be home tonight. I'll probably stay with Sasha. She needs me. Please don't call. I'll call you tomorrow.*

I tossed the note out as I drove back to work.

CHAPTER SIXTEEN

THE STOLI was calming my nerves, but it wasn't helping my ability to use the fucking phone. I generally got the number I wanted on the second attempt, though sometimes it took me three or four. When I got home to our very quiet house, I called Sasha again. Linda wasn't there, she told me. She had no idea where she was. For some reason, I believed her. Then I made up a Linda call list: friends; family (just her mother and a younger sister); hotels (in town and in Boston). I even put my father down. Who knew? Maybe she was staying with my folks. She wasn't, of course. I didn't want to say that I was trying to find my wife. That I didn't have a clue where she was and that I was getting scared. That wouldn't do at all. I was Danny Martell, supposedly a tough cop. Every mutt and hustler in Providence knew that they had to talk to me just so. So why the fuck was I so antsy?

The story I used (except for the hotel, where I checked under both her maiden and married names) was that I was thinking about throwing a surprise party for Linda (her birthday was next month), and I wanted to know if they could make it. I figured that if any of them knew where she was, I would sense it in how they answered. Most said they'd love to come, and those who couldn't sounded truly unhappy about it. Wherever Linda was, no one I called that night knew a thing.

I don't know when I went to sleep, because I passed out. The next morning I awoke on the couch, my mouth tasting like I had gargled the rug. After I brushed my teeth (twice) and had some coffee, I called Linda's office. It was just past eight, but she always got there by seven thirty at the latest, even on a Sunday, if there was a big project in the works. After six rings, I got her voice mail. I threw on yesterday's clothes and left. I had arranged with Alex to pick him up, and he was waiting outside his house.

"You're almost twenty minutes late, my friend."

"Sorry," I mumbled.

And then I noticed two livid scratches that started below his ear and snaked down his neck, almost to his chin.

"What happened to you?"

"Samantha. I guess my cat didn't like the lady I brought home last night. And you don't look so hot yourself. What's up?"

I drove a few blocks before I could answer.

"Linda didn't sleep at home last night. That's the second night in a row."

"Fight?"

I nodded.

"Where'd she go?"

"I called everybody I could think of. I don't have a clue."

"Jesus."

I stopped at a red light.

"Where we going?" he asked.

"To work."

"Fuck that. You have to go to her office."

"But Kitty—"

"Linda is more important. Turn the light on, and let's move it."

When I got there a couple of minutes later, Alex stayed in the car. The receptionist told me that Linda had still not gotten in. In fact, she whispered to me, there were two men in the reception area who were waiting for her. This was her second appointment. The first had left already. Though Linda used a PalmPilot, she also kept an old-fashioned appointment book. I went into her office and opened it: three meetings in the morning, a business lunch, and two more meetings in the afternoon. I couldn't tell how important they were, but there was no way she would miss them without calling in.

I walked to the window and looked out over the harbor. It was a great view, but I didn't see anything. I felt cold and empty. I was having trouble catching my breath. I dropped down into Linda's chair. It looked like it had been designed by NASA. It was done in soft black leather and, I think, cost a couple thousand bucks. I looked at her desk. Everything was in perfect order: pens lined up on one side of the leather IN and OUT boxes, a stack of yellow lined pads on the other. I almost felt as if she were there in the room. I don't know how long I sat there before Alex walked into the office.

"What's happening?"

"Nothing."

"I don't like this at all. You've got to file a report."

"I don't want to think that way."

"She's probably fine, but you have to play it by the book."

"I guess you're right."

"Danny, let's get out of here and get some coffee. We have to talk."

"About what?"

"Wake up, my man. Your wife. Linda. That's the only thing on your plate that matters. Let's go."

CHAPTER SEVENTEEN

I DIDN'T file the MPR until an hour before I clocked out Sunday evening. If you asked me what I did all day, I'd answer by handing you a blank piece of paper. Alex made me go back to Linda's office to get her call log, which I should have taken when I was there in the morning. Using it, I made a bunch of calls but turned up nothing. I kept telling myself that she was fine, probably holed up in a hotel somewhere, maybe New York, watching videos and eating crème caramel, her favorite dessert. I wanted to scream out that she had made her point, that I was an angry, paranoid piece of shit and all I wanted was for her to come home. Lesson learned. Just give me another chance, baby. It was a long, long day. I walked through it like I had a bad head cold and was doing a shitty audition for the part of Danny Martell.

Alex wanted me to have dinner with him: "Come on. We'll grab a meal and catch a movie. Something loud and mindless. That won't be hard to find. It'll be good for you." But I knew that I had to go home, and he didn't press me when I said no. I wasn't home more than five minutes when the front doorbell rang. I rushed down the stairs. It was Jimmy Warden. We hugged, and I led him into the kitchen. Jimmy loved his lager, and I always kept a couple of bottles of his favorite in the fridge.

"Great to see you, Jimmy. What's up?"

"Can the shit, Danny. Kitty told me the whole Linda story. What the fuck is going on?"

"I wish I knew," I said.

"How long since you last saw her?"

"Friday night. We had a fight, and she didn't sleep at home. I talked to her yesterday on the phone, but I didn't see her at all. She didn't sleep at home again."

"Kitty thought she'd only been gone one night."

"I guess the Captain wasn't in her *Jeopardy* mode," I said, trying to smile.

"This is no time to try to be funny. Don't crack wise with me like your friend Alex. Now give me the whole story, Danny. Everything. Right from the beginning."

Jimmy was always there when I needed him, so I wasn't surprised that he came over as soon as he heard about Linda.

"You've left something out."

"I gave you everything, Jimmy. Honest."

"Don't lie. There's more. What is it?"

So I told him. I hadn't told anyone, even Alex, about my suspicions that Linda was having an affair, but I told Jimmy.

"What do you think?" I asked him.

He took a long swallow from the bottle and then carefully placed it back on the table.

"Has she ever done anything like this before?"

"Never."

"Did she take clothes with her when she left?"

"Whatever she could fit into a small shoulder bag. Not much."

"Have you checked the hospitals?"

"Both here and Boston. Alex did New York."

"Did she take her car?"

"It's still in the driveway."

"Did she withdraw a large amount out of her checking account?"

"No. She didn't even take her checkbook with her."

"Her health good?"

"Perfect. She had a three-day thing at the Mayo a couple of months ago."

Jimmy stood up and walked over to the window.

"You know, Danny," he said as he came over to where I was sitting and put his hands on my shoulders, "even after going through the whole thing with Bonnie, I think I'm still an optimist. There's plenty of reasons to be worried about Linda, I won't deny that, but you can't stop believing that this is going to work out."

"I pray you're right, Jimmy."

After Jimmy got another beer, we both realized that we were hungry. I wasn't up to eating at Martelli's, for all the obvious reasons, so we walked a couple of blocks to The Sombrero, a pretty good Mexican place that served world-class margaritas. We started with guacamole that a waitress made at the table using a large stone mortar and pestle to grind the avocado into paste.

"That's a great kitchen you guys put in," said Jimmy, taking a long drink from his Corona. "You still cooking a lot?"

"Not as much as I'd like to. Linda really puts in the hours."

"Well, that's what paid for the kitchen."

"Don't I know it."

"Bonnie was a hell of a cook. Pot roast, clam chowder, corned beef—you name it, she could turn it out."

"I remember lots of great meals at your place, Jimmy. I was brought up with good food, both at the house and at the family joint, and I know how important it is."

"Amen to that."

I ordered another margarita. I was beginning to feel almost normal.

"You've got to come over soon. I'll cook up some chicken *scarpariello*. It's my grandmother's recipe. You loved it last time you were over."

"Give me a date, and I'll be there."

As I reached into my jacket for my datebook, my cell phone rang.

"Martell here."

"I just called Alex." It was Captain Kitty. "We got another one. Right off the bike trail near Pollack Street. I'm heading there now."

"On my way."

I threw a twenty and a ten on the table and got up.

"Got to go, Jimmy."

"Is this that angel thing Kitty told me about?"

I nodded.

"Hope you don't mind company. I think I'll come along."

The bike trail had been created fifteen years before by paving over a long spur of the old B&O railroad tracks. It ran almost eight miles and was heavily used by both walkers and bicyclists. Of course, at night it was deserted. There were some houses that faced the trail, but most of it was thickly lined with trees and brush.

It was the usual scene when we got there ten minutes later: five squad cars, lights circling, blocking access to the trail; a clutch of the morbidly curious from the neighborhood. I headed toward the flash of a camera signaling where the body was. Jimmy was at my side. I was fifty feet away when Captain Kitty came out of nowhere and grabbed my arm.

"No, Danny. Stay here."

"What's up?"

"There's something I have to tell you."

Then Alex was by my other side, his hands tight on my upper arm.

"Don't go there, Danny. We have to talk to you."

"What the fuck is going on?" I said, trying to shake their hands off me.

"Danny," said Captain Kitty, "let's go back to my car."

"Take it easy, buddy," said Jimmy, his arm now on my shoulder.

I spun around and faced them.

"Why are you stopping me?"

Kitty stepped close enough to kiss me and said, "It's Linda."

CHAPTER EIGHTEEN

I **DON'T** remember a lot about that night, but I think Jimmy drove me home in my car. Alex showed up later, maybe an hour or so, with Captain Kitty. Jimmy put two bottles (vodka and scotch) and a bunch of glasses on the large marble table in front of the sofa. Then he brought out an ice bucket. For a long while, the loudest noise in the room was the clink of the cubes dancing in the glasses.

I woke up the next morning in my bed, or rather, on top of it. Clothes still on, though my shoes were off. It took me a good ten minutes to brush my teeth and comb my hair. I found Jimmy asleep in the guest room and Alex on the sofa. By the time I had a pot of coffee ready, they were both up.

"You okay?" asked Alex.

I wanted to answer, but I couldn't.

"Your father called. They'll be over here in an hour. Also your brother."

"I want to go to the morgue."

"That can wait, Danny," said Jimmy.

"No, it can't. I've got to see her."

"You're not ready yet," said Alex.

"I'm as ready now as I ever will be."

"A lot of people will be coming here soon."

"Leave the door open."

I don't know how many times I had been to the morgue—seventy-five, maybe a hundred—but the thing that always got to me was the smell: sort of a cross between a gym locker and bug spray. I almost felt like a perp, with Alex on one side and Jimmy on the other, as we walked in. We didn't have to wait long before we were led into one of the storage rooms. They always reminded me of a strange type of showroom, the merchandise hidden behind metal doors. The two of them got closer to me as the attendant opened it and rolled out Linda's body.

He pulled the cover down, and there she was. She didn't look bad. A bruise above her right eyebrow and a small cut on her chin. They were unsuccessfully covered with makeup.

I reached down and placed my hand on her cheek.

"Hey, baby." Jimmy and Alex tightened their grip on my elbows. "I love you. You know that, don't you? No one's going to hurt you anymore." I bent down and kissed her.

"We should go, Danny," said Jimmy in a whisper.

"I don't want to leave her here."

"We'll come back later."

I let them lead me out. Alex's car was in front, the red stick-on whirling on the roof.

"Where we going?" I asked.

"Back to your place."

"No. Take me to the scene."

"There's nothing there except tape," said Alex.

"Just take me there. Please."

The forensic people had come and gone, and the area had been swept. All that remained were the bands of yellow tape that corralled the area. There was a slight breeze, and the tape made a strange humming sound as it fluttered. With my duennas bracketing me, I lifted up the tape and walked toward the place, marked by small white flags, where Linda's body had been found.

"There's nothing to see here, Danny," said Jimmy as he slipped his arm over my shoulder.

I walked around the area, about twice the size of a pitcher's mound, careful not to step on the spray-painted outline of Linda's body. Why? Was it superstition? Whatever. I just couldn't step on it. A bicyclist and a Rollerblader slipped by on the path above us. Alex had parked the car at the edge of the trees about a hundred yards away. That was obviously where Linda's killer had come from. He had carried her all the way from there. Had he sat in his car for a long time until the area was absolutely quiet? Probably. Just him and Linda.

"Your whole family is probably at your house by now." That was Alex. "I think you should get back."

"He's right, Danny."

I walked up to the bike path. In the distance I saw a woman pushing a baby carriage.

"This is not like the other places," I said, almost to myself.

"Yes, it is," Alex answered. "Secluded. No traffic. Hardly any lights."

"The others had absolutely no light. And I bet there were a few people here at all hours."

"They're going to put everyone on this, Danny. They'll get the guy."

"Jimmy's right. Kitty's going to throw the whole department on it."

"Yeah. I guess she will. But there's one thing she can't do." Jimmy and Alex stared at me. "She won't bring Linda back."

The house was jammed. I was embraced as soon as I opened the door. My father kissed me on the lips! His face was awash with tears. Then it was my mother and grandmother.

"Oh, my poor baby," said my mother, sobbing. "What will you do?"

"It'll be okay, Mom."

My grandmother's English, which was problematic at best, now retreated not just to Italian, but to the dialect of her native village. I could make out only an occasional word here or there. I was pushed into the kitchen, where my uncle was unpacking bags of food from the restaurant. I sat down, or was shoved into a chair, and, strangely, I felt hungry. Really hungry.

Plate after plate was set down in front of me—chicken, pasta, meatballs, salad—and I cleaned every one. This seemed to comfort my family.

The doorbell rang all the time, like a metronome on speed. A stream of cops did laps around my chair in the kitchen. Some patted my shoulder, and most gave me a hug. Then there were people from Linda's office. Guys in suits and ties and a few women, all of them crying. I got shoulder pats from the men and kisses from the ladies. Then there were the neighbors, and the owners of the stores I shopped at. Santino Volpe came with a huge leg of lamb that led to a discussion between him and my uncle on the perfect way to cook it. Later the Flea paid a visit with his girlfriend, who was also cornrowed. The rows definitely looked better on her.

"I don't know what to say, Danny." I looked up. It was Molly Juste. She still had on her Al Forno's name tag. She must have come straight from the restaurant. "Just be strong."

"I'll be okay, Molly."

"I know you will."

The house started to thin out as we slipped into the night. My family all wanted to spend the night with me, but I told them I wanted to be alone. The same went for Alex and Jimmy. I moved from the kitchen to the living room and then finally to the bedroom, when the last one, Jimmy, left.

If I dreamed, I can't recall anything. I do remember that in the middle of the night I reached across the bed to Linda's pillow. I did that every night. I just liked to touch her hair. Of course, there wasn't anything to touch.

CHAPTER NINETEEN

LINDA'S MOTHER, Jen, and her sister, Meg, arrived Tuesday morning. All we could do was fall into each other's arms and sob. Jen had moved to West Palm Beach the year before, so she had no objection to my having the funeral in Providence. Since Linda was raised Episcopalian, I had Alex call Father Coles, who agreed to officiate the service. I knew it wouldn't be easy for my grand-mother, who was still recovering from our getting married by a judge and had never stepped inside a house of worship other than a Catholic church.

I invited Jen and Meg to stay at my house, which opened the floodgates for my family to move in, too. They took over every available flat space. The only place left for my brother was the sauna. My parents wanted Linda to have an open coffin, but I said no.

"But she was so beautiful," my father said.

"She'll always be beautiful, Dad."

About midafternoon I pulled Jimmy Warden aside.

"I want you to give me a lift to Tomei's."

"Tomei's?"

"The funeral parlor," I whispered. "I have to see her."

"My car's down the block."

We didn't talk as Jimmy drove toward Federal Hill. I didn't know what he was thinking, but the loop that was running in my mind was driving him two years before to look at Bonnie.

"You know, I'm here for you, Danny," he said as we pulled into the parking lot. "I hate the expression 'twenty-four/seven,' but I'll always be there."

I just reached over and squeezed his shoulder.

Why do funeral directors always rub their hands together? That's what Fred Tomei was doing as he led us down to the basement of the funeral home. The coffin he took us to was big, dark, heavy, and certainly expensive—a sign that my father had called this shot. He raised the lid and then backed away like a servant in an Elizabethan play.

Jimmy put his arm around my shoulder.

Linda looked surprisingly good, though in a way she looked like someone else. Like a portrait based on a description. Her hair was perfect. Too perfect. I leaned down and kissed her forehead.

"I love you, baby. I always will."

I let Jimmy turn me back toward the stairs. Moments later we were in his car.

"Drink?"

"What do you think?" I answered.

CHAPTER TWENTY

I **DON'T** remember much about the service. The church was packed. A ton of TV and press outside. The same at my house. The Angel story had broken. Big-time. It was now *the* story in Providence. Made the front page in Boston, too.

The best part of the service was the organ and the chorus. Linda's sister, two guys from her firm, and my father spoke. My father broke up four times. Would he be this distraught if I had died? It was a nice thought, but I doubted it.

Afterward, back at the house, there were even more people than the day before. Loads of food and booze, tears and hugging. Tim Rackmill, one of the partners in Linda's firm, told me the company had given her a large insurance policy. Two million. I told him I wanted her mother and sister to get it. I don't know how many days it went on, but, finally, I was alone again.

I camped out on the couch. Sweats and T-shirt. The phone rang a lot, but I didn't pick it up. I could hear the messages. My brother asking me to catch a movie with him. Captain Kitty telling me to take my time. She knew what I was going through. "You're strong," she said. "Never forget that." Alex saying the same thing.

I kept the TV on all the time: ESPN and Oprah; the Weather Channel and Wolf Blitzer (was that his real name?). There was a hundred pounds of food in the fridge. Every once in a while I made myself a sandwich. Most of the time I didn't finish it. The doorbell rang a lot, but I never opened it. I'd just use the remote to up the sound to block out the ringing. Then (I didn't even know what day it was) there was a banging on my front door. Real pounding. And it wouldn't stop. The remote didn't help. I heard someone shouting.

"I know you're in there, Martell! Open the fucking door before..."

It was Jimmy Warden. I knew that if I didn't let him in, he would, in fact, break it down.

"Jesus, you look like hell. And you stink. Get the fuck upstairs and take a shower. Make yourself look like a human being. And then burn those clothes. Where's the scotch? I need a drink."

The shower actually felt good. When I went downstairs, Jimmy was in the kitchen, doing the dishes.

"This place is a fucking pigsty. Take off the dishes that I've rinsed and put them in the dishwasher. When we finish we're going to get the fuck out of here."

Jimmy drove first to Larsen's, a pool hall on the west side of the Brown campus. We used to play there a lot when I first joined the force. Nine-ball. Back then I was pretty good, and I don't think Jimmy ever beat me. That was then. Jimmy hadn't gotten much better, but I was truly lousy.

"Get your head into the game, Danny. You play like Al Hibbler."

"Who's that?"

"I guess you're too young. He was a great singer. And he was blind."

After a few more games where I only got worse, Jimmy took me to the Salsa Garden, a Mexican storefront restaurant on the other side of town. As the waitress set down our plates, I actually felt hungry for the first time in days.

"When are you going back to work?"

"I don't know. Next week, maybe."

"That's no good. You have to go back tomorrow. Not next week. Not even the day after tomorrow. Understood?"

"I don't know if I can, Jimmy. I feel so empty. Lost, really."

"I know, Danny. But you have work to do. You've got to start living again."

"I need a few more days."

"That's not the answer. You'll go back tomorrow, Monday. You have to find the creep that killed Linda."

"I'll try."

"Don't give me this 'try' shit. Just go in. I'll be there, too. Kitty's giving me an office to use."

"Why?"

"There's an old case that I want to look into."

"Do I know it?"

"No. It didn't even take place here. It happened over ten years ago. In Litchfield County, Connecticut. There are resemblances to the Angel business we have here. I'll tell you more tomorrow. In the station house!"

CHAPTER TWENTY-ONE

I GUESS Jimmy has a lot of influence over me, because I got up the next morning, after finally giving up my home on the couch and sleeping in my bed, and went to work. I also did some other things that I hadn't done in a while: I shaved for the first time since the funeral, four days before. Amazing. And then I realized that I was on the four-to-twelve shift. That gave me some time to clean up the place a bit. The most important thing I did was open the windows. Jimmy was right: the place did stink.

I called Alex and arranged to pick him up at the Little War Shoppe. Aside from the station house, this was the place where Alex spent most of his time. The store was owned by Seymour Janson, who was also a member of Alex's war-gaming group. Janson was a short, round man with a Chernobyl red face, whose first gear was high excitability that went way up from there. According to Alex there was no store in all of the country that stocked as many toy soldiers and books on war gaming. The place was crammed with thousands of little gleaming metal figures.

As usual, when I got there, Alex and Seymour were having an argument.

"You're out of your mind, Larch!" shouted Seymour, whose voice certainly could be heard on the street. "The Seventh Illinois always wore a blue tunic with black belts. I'd show it to you, but I sold my last squad the other day to a guy from Delaware."

"I'll prove it to you next Tuesday. I have a couple at my place. You're confusing the Seventh with the Connecticut Twelfth."

This went on for another ten minutes until Alex saw me pointing to my watch.

"You lost some weight," he said when we got in the car.

"So what. That's the least of it. And I'm sure I'll put it back on in a few weeks."

The first person to come into our office was Captain Kitty. I saw her give a nod to Alex.

"I think I'll go and get some coffee. You want any?" he asked.

"What I said to you in your house will always stand. I'm here for you, Danny. We all are."

"I know that, Cap."

I wanted to give her a hug. Here? In the station house? Fuck it! I went over to her and held her tight.

"I don't know what to say," I finally got out.

"Neither do I."

Later, when we were in the car heading over to the church to see the other volunteers, Alex started to say something, coughed a bit, and then stopped.

"What the fuck's wrong with you?"

"What I want to say is not easy."

"Just say it."

"It's about Linda."

"What?"

"There are some inconsistencies. Maybe she wasn't killed by the same creep who did the first two."

"You're wrong. The guy who did the others killed Linda. That's who we have to get."

CHAPTER TWENTY-TWO

AFTER I woke up, it took me a few minutes to realize that it was Saturday. *Congratulations, Martell, you made it through the week.* Alex and I had put a lot of mileage on our car, talked to a ton of people, and turned up nothing. Absolutely nada. Thankfully the TV and newspaper people were now onto something else: a couple in Cranston had been discovered trying to sell a kidney (on the Internet, of course). What made the story hot was that the organ that they were peddling belonged to their fourteen-year-old son. The media were calling them Mom and Pop Transplant.

The phone, as usual, was ringing a lot. My mother had called me three times, and it was only noon. Why wasn't I coming to the family lunch tomorrow? I just wasn't up to it, I had said. Then I got a call from my father. The last time he called was ten years ago, after his car was stolen. I guess it was the only time he thought there was something good about having a son who was a cop.

"Danny, please come. We need you and you need us."

"It's not the right time, Dad."

"Yes, it is. I want to see you."

"All I can say is I'll try."

"I loved Linda, son. But I love you, too. I know what you're going through. This is a time for us to be together."

Mission accomplished. I told him I'd be there. But before that we both did a solid three minutes of sobbing. I had to wash my face after I hung up. Jesus.

About an hour later, the doorbell rang. Now that I had at least one foot back in the world, I hesitated only a moment before opening the door.

"Hi, Danny." It was Molly Juste. "Can I come in?"

"Of course," I finally got out. I'd forgotten how great she looked.

She was carrying two large shopping bags.

"Where's the kitchen?"

"Down the hall, on your left."

She put the bags on the kitchen table and started to unpack.

"Hope you have an appetite. There are some great goodies in here. Courtesy of Al Forno's."

My appetite was zero, since I had had breakfast an hour before, but I didn't want to disappoint her.

"Where are the plates?"

The food was so good that I actually ate quite a bit. Our talk at first was halting and awkward. She, thankfully, stayed away from asking how I was doing. Molly asked about Bernie Sands and was happy to hear that the DA thought the case against him was a lock. We talked about her acting. She wanted to go to New York in a year or two.

"Did your partner tell you he took me out to dinner?"

"No. When was that?"

"A few nights after we took those staged photos. That was after asking me out two or three times a day. He's a very persistent fellow."

"Did you have fun?"

"It wasn't bad, but he's not my type. I know what his type is."

"And what is that?"

"You're his partner and friend. I don't have to tell you."

"I guess you're right."

A few minutes later, I poured each of us a glass of wine. I didn't think about it. I didn't even ask her if she wanted any. I just did it. I didn't want her to leave. The next thing I knew, I was laughing. Molly Juste was a very funny woman. I hadn't laughed in a long time. It felt good.

"You should stop by Al Forno sometime."

"Do I get a discount?"

"Oh, I'd say more than that."

Whether it was intentional or not, I loved the double entendre. Then I realized that I was turned on. A boner in the making. That's not what a grieving husband is supposed to feel. I wrestled with it for a while, and grief won out. When she left, I kissed her chastely on the cheek. She, in turn, gave me a hug, fairly tight and long. It felt good. I knew I shouldn't be thinking this, but I wanted to see Molly again.

CHAPTER TWENTY-THREE

THE FAMILY lunch at my uncle's restaurant the next afternoon was like that old comedy line about watching paint dry. My father, for the first time since I graduated law school, sat next to me. He was all over me. The only thing he didn't do was cut up the veal and feed me. And, of course, the family chorus repeatedly echoed the lines, "Why aren't you eating more, Danny? Is something wrong?" I didn't want to get into any arguments, so I reluctantly took a forkful of each of the myriad dishes that circled the table.

"Take this," said my aunt Theresa, thrusting a file card into my hand.

I looked at it. The name Dr. Morris Blatt was printed in large block letters, along with an address and phone number.

"What's this?" I asked.

"He's the best grief therapist in the state. He treated my best friend, Dottie. Jimmy, her husband, was killed when his dump truck went into the bay. He was a lovely guy. That was four years ago."

I folded the card and put it into my pocket.

"Thanks, Aunt Theresa. I'll call him this week."

"Call him Monday. He can really help you. I've seen what he's done for Dottie. And he's not expensive."

It wasn't easy, but I left early. For some reason I found myself driving to the station house. Alex and I weren't scheduled to work the four-to-twelve on Sunday, and there wasn't anything I needed. I had copies of all our interviews at the house. I went into my office and checked my answering machine. There were two from the Flea. Had I talked to the DA? A couple of others from people I had tried to talk to who lived by Norris Park. I had left my card in their mailbox. As I left, I walked by the office Jimmy was using. And, no surprise, he was there.

"What are you up to, Jimmy?"

"Remember those murders I told you about in Litchfield County?"

"The women. About eleven years ago?"

"That's it. Never found the guy. Took place over a four-year period. I haven't turned up much. But I have a hunch there might be a tie to our guy here. I want to go up there. Maybe this week. Would you like to come with me?"

"Sure. I think I can do it on Thursday."

"Sounds good. It'll take two and a half to three to get there. Let's say we leave by eight."

"Fine with me."

"Danny, why don't you sit down a minute. There's something else I want to talk to you about." There was only one chair in his office, so I didn't have to think about where to sit. "You're not going to like what I'm going to say to you." Jimmy took out a folder from the desk drawer and dropped it onto the desk. "You know what's in that?"

"I have no idea."

"It's the coroner's report on Linda. Have you read it?"

"No. And I don't want to read it. Where the fuck are you going, Jimmy?"

"The coroner thinks Linda died from severe blunt trauma to the head."

"I smell Alex dancing around here."

"I don't know what you're talking about."

"You're going to tell me that Linda wasn't killed by the Angel, right?"

"That's right. But what does Alex have to do with this?"

"That's his theory, too."

"Well, for once I'm going to have to agree with him."

"And you're also going to tell me that the makeup that the creep used was not like what was put on the first two."

"That's right."

"Well, maybe the fucking department store ran out of his favorite shade. Or maybe he was in a rush and had to use some other kind. Jimmy, you're too smart to fall for this shit. Linda was killed by the same nut job who killed the first two. When we get him, we'll have the guy who took my wife. If you don't mind, Jimmy, it's Sunday, and I believe I have the day off."

CHAPTER TWENTY-FOUR

TOGETHER WITH Hughes and Miley from the Seventh, we spent Monday afternoon talking to every shop owner on the two main hooker-pickup streets in the city. One of them, an old man who had a luggage store, saw a guy in a silver Lexus hit a hooker and then push her into his car on the day we found the second victim. He even took down the license plate number. For about twenty minutes we thought we finally had something. But the DMV told us that the car was owned by Teddy Boy Willis, a well-known pimp. Teddy Boy was just doing his job, keeping his lady in line.

"You know something?" Alex asked me as we drove back to the station house.

"What?"

"We haven't developed a fucking thing. We don't even have a vague idea what this guy is up to. Like, why is he dressing them like angels? What is he trying to tell us?"

"He's a sick fuck who'll keep doing it until we get him. He's another serial killer who always wanted to be a costume designer."

"Very funny."

"I thought so."

Of course, I didn't. My head was, at best, sitting where it was supposed to be. I guess it looked normal. But it was very fucked up. I had pulled a book from a pile in the living room the night before. It was called *I Never Had a Chance to Say Goodbye*. After Linda's death, I had received a lot of wine, flowers, and books. All of them, except for three copies of *The Prophet*, dealt with grieving and mourning. I learned that grieving preceded mourning. I certainly was in the former mode. I'm sure the book had lots of good advice on how to deal with what I was going through, but I gave up before I finished the preface. I knew I had to battle this alone. And I knew that it would take time. A lot of time.

"Well, do you want to come along with me after we sign out?"

"What?"

"I asked you if you wanted to go with me to see Brooks Shelby."

"Who?"

"We met at the church. Shelby was one of the volunteers in the outreach program."

"Which one was he?"

"He's the conservator at the RISD Museum. The other guy—Arnie—owns a used-car lot."

"Why the fuck do you want to see him?"

"He's going to show me around this exhibition they have on battle scenes from the Renaissance to World War Two. I've read a couple of reviews. It sounds great."

"Great for you."

"Come on. What else are you going to do after I drop you off? Sit on the couch and watch *Judge Judy*?"

"Her show ends at six."

"I hope that was a joke."

"I think it was," I said, trying to smile.

I decided to go with Alex because he was right—all I was going to do when I got to my place was sit on the couch and watch TV. And, of course, have a vodka or two and a couple of beers.

"Detective Larch," said Shelby as we walked into his office. "And it's good to see you, Detective Martell. I didn't know you were coming, too."

Shelby's office was small but seemed smaller with all the art on the walls. The top of his desk and bookcase were crowded with small sculptures.

"Neither did I. My partner is very persuasive."

"Are you involved in war gaming, too?"

"Not so you'd notice it."

"Well, I suggest we start out with a few paintings of battles from the late Renaissance and then move quickly so we can get to the Civil War. I know that's of particular interest to Detective Larch. What battle are you fighting now?"

"The Battle of the Wilderness."

"Well, you're in luck. We have a magnificent oil from a private collection in Savannah. It's stunning."

The painting was terrific, as were at least a dozen others. For a small arts college, Rhode Island School of Design had an impressive collection. And though Shelby had curated the exhibition, he stopped at other works that were not included and commented on them, too. When we finished our tour, he led us back to his office for a drink.

"I have wine, both red and white. Vodka and scotch, too. I know it sounds a bit prissy, but I'm going to have a sherry. I have one that's quite dry. Thirty years old. It's really good."

Strangely enough, I took the sherry, and Shelby was right.

"Have you made any progress on those killings?" he asked.

"We really can't talk about it, Shelby," said Alex. "It's an ongoing investigation."

"I'm sorry. I shouldn't have asked."

"No problem," Alex said. "How long have you been here at the museum?"

"It'll be three years in November. Before that I taught art history at Hotchkiss."

"The private school?"

"Yes, it's in Connecticut."

"Why'd you switch?" I asked.

"Two reasons: money and I prefer city living. By the way, I think it would be useful if you left a copy of those photos at the shelter. We get new women coming in all the time. One might have known them."

"We'll drop them off tomorrow," I said as I stood up and followed Alex out of the office.

"Oh, Detective Martell," he said softly, placing his hand on my shoulder, "all of us want you to know how sorry we are about your wife. We found out that she supported the ACLU, so we decided to make a contribution in her memory."

I tried to thank him, but I knew I would start slobbering if I stayed there a moment longer. I turned and almost ran to catch up with Alex.

CHAPTER TWENTY-FIVE

THE NEXT day was more of the same: talking to people who lived near the park, checking out mutts that had recent assault records, the usual shit. All we turned up was a decent Indian place to have lunch. Captain Kitty didn't want me working on Linda's case, so she assigned Greco and Farber to head that up. She added four guys from the Fifth and three from Central Homicide to back them.

When I got home, I did my usual stations of the cross. First I went to the freezer and poured a cryogenic Ketel One into a chilled glass. Then I went to the answering machine. The number 11 flashed on the small message window. Since Linda's death, my call popularity had gone way up. Two were from my mother. She'd found a good cleaning woman for me, and did I want some osso buco tonight? She had cooked an extra portion for me. Just say the word, and she'd drop it off. Then there was my father. Was I up for a Celtics game this weekend? Two calls each from my aunts and one from my brother. Linda's mother thanked me (the fifth time) for giving her the insurance money. And then there was a call from Molly Juste: "Danny, I know it's a last-minute thing, but I just realized that tonight is my free-meal night here at Al Forno. Once a month they give us a free dinner for two. I'd love it if you'd join me. Call me on my cell."

I didn't listen to the rest of the message. I quickly banged out Molly's number. She picked it up on the first ring.

"Hi. This is Molly."

"Is my seat still empty? You haven't invited someone else?"

"You got in just under the wire, Danny. How does eight sound?"

I got to the restaurant a half hour early. I was wearing a dark blue Turnbull & Asser shirt and a tan Armani jacket, both Christmas presents from Linda that were favorites of mine. The bar was crowded, but I found a seat at the end next to a woman with short, spiky blond hair and a low-cut blouse that left nothing to the imagination. She was drinking a noxious-looking green drink that looked like something that had leaked out of Love Canal.

"It's called a Grasshopper," she volunteered, after seeing me stare at it. "It's made with crème de menthe."

"It sure looks it."

I ordered a chilled Grey Goose with a twist.

"What's Grey Goose?" she asked.

"It's a type of vodka."

"Why do they call it that? Is there goose feathers or something like that in it?"

I was dreading her next question when I saw Molly look into the bar for a moment. I mumbled something to the Grasshopper woman, tossed a few bills on the bar, and headed out. Molly was looking into one of the dining rooms when I tapped her on the shoulder.

"Hi. It's your mystery guest," I whispered.

She wheeled around and hugged me. She gave me a kiss on each cheek.

"I picked out a great table for us. It's quiet, and we can see the river."

I followed as she crossed the room. All the waitress and busboys smiled and waved at her. A bottle of red wine was on the table, and I noticed next to it a glass filled with a clear liquid. There was a curl of lemon peel floating on top.

"Is that—"

"Grey Goose. That's what you drink, right?"

"How did you know?"

"Remember, I was in your kitchen. And if I can remember a part in a play, the name of a vodka is a cinch."

Gwen, our waitress, opened the wine. I poured some for Molly and then clinked my glass against hers.

"First, a thank-you. I can't think of a place that I'd rather be. I know there's a long list of guys you could have invited, and I'm flattered and happy that you picked me."

"Actually the list is quite short. Practically nonexistent. What's second?"

"The second is that, in all the years I've been a cop, nobody who I met through—I guess I could say 'business'—has ever invited me out to dinner."

"Well, I'm happy you accepted."

I asked Molly to do the ordering, and the food was terrific. The first course was a salad of mâche, heirloom tomatoes, and corn with a dressing so good that I asked Molly to get me the recipe. I had taken only a bite or two from our second course, veal piccata with wild mushrooms, when my pager went off. It was Captain Kitty.

"Molly, I have to make a call, and I don't have my cell with me. I'll be back in a minute."

That was a lie. It was department policy that we always had to have our cell with us. But this was a call that I didn't want Molly, or anyone else, listening in on. Captain Kitty's message was short and scary: "Danny—call me ASAP. We have another Angel."

CHAPTER TWENTY-SIX

EVEN THOUGH I slapped the flasher onto the roof, it took me almost twenty minutes to get to Indian Point Park. I ran into both a fire at a 7-Eleven and a bad crash between a truck and a bus on Armitage Road. The park hugged the shoreline of the harbor, and a lot of people used it in the summer to put small sailboats into the water. This time I was the second to arrive. Captain Kitty was just getting out of her car when I pulled up.

"Have you talked to Alex or Jimmy?" she asked.

Before I could answer, a young cop walked over to us.

"Captain, it's this way," he said. There were two others behind him. We followed them into a small knot of saplings and high grass that was a hundred feet from the shore. "The ME and the tech people should be here soon."

They had taped off the area and placed a couple of battery-powered lamps on tripods around the body. The light was strong, and the victim seemed to be staring up at them as if she were sunbathing at the beach. She was white and looked to be in her thirties. The wings were there, but they were completely different from the others. They were small and pointed and made out of red velvet. The makeup was heavy and made her look almost clownish.

"This doesn't look right," I told Kitty.

"Let's wait for the others. We don't want to jump too fast."

The rest of the team arrived within ten minutes, and Alex and Jimmy right after them. The four of us walked over to our cars and waited while the others did their work.

"This one is strange," said Jimmy.

"How so?" asked the Captain.

"Come on, Kitty. I don't have to spell it out."

"Maybe you should."

"Jesus. It looks and feels a lot different."

"Why does one have to look exactly like the others? Maybe he's in a red-velvet phase now."

I looked over at Alex, who was lighting a cigarette. "When did you get back to that fucking terrible hobby?"

"A couple of days ago."

Al Mason, the ME, walked over.

"Well?" asked Kitty.

"This one was choked by hand, not strangled with a rope. There are prints on the neck. And bruises around the body. Especially the back."

"When did it happen?"

"Maybe three, four days ago."

"And the others?"

"Twenty-four hours. Forty-eight tops. And there's something else."

"Let me guess."

"You'll never get this one."

"Let me try. She—"

"You're wrong already. It's not a she. What you have is a 'she-male' on your hands."

"Jesus!" said Jimmy.

The four of us drove over to Reid's, an all-night diner on Fulton, for coffee.

"I hate those two words. We really have to move fast now," said Kitty as she stirred her coffee.

"What do you mean?" I asked.

"Copycat. We have someone else working out there now. I have to talk to Al Frisch first thing in the morning."

"The metro guy at the *Journal*?" asked Alex.

"Yeah."

"Why him?"

"He's the guy who runs the Angel coverage. I'll give him enough on this piece of business so he doesn't play it up as an Angel killing. Another one will get this case back on page one. I have to convince him that this doesn't have anything to do with the others."

"Think he'll buy it?" Jimmy asked.

"He'd better. Now, I'm hungry. I could use a fruit salad. Anybody else game?"

"If you let us go the ham-and-egg route," said Alex, "we'll all sign on."

CHAPTER TWENTY-SEVEN

I PICKED Alex up at seven thirty the next morning. We spent two hours at the station, going through what had been dug up since last night.

It didn't take long for this case to get a tag—it was a tradition in the department. Charlie Sopkin came up with this one, and it was inspired: Madame Surprise.

There were nine of us assigned to the new case. Unlike the other murders, we had a lot to start working with. A man who was taking his boat out of the water had spotted a car (a white, fairly new Tahoe) that was parked near where we found the victim, and he had even gotten down three numbers of the plate (which, he was positive, had a Rhode Island tag). There was a good partial print on the victim's neck and excellent impressions of both a shoe and a sneaker. It looked like we were looking for a copycat team. Best of all, we had an ID on the victim. Real name was Thomas Michael Barton. "She" went under the name of Tina Barnes, lived 24/7 as a woman, and had half a dozen priors for soliciting.

Tina had a bad habit of not telling her johns that she packed equipment. It made some of them very angry. This led to a number of beatings. A few were serious. We divided the workload and then set out. Alex and I knew that this was one that we would wrap up fairly soon. Typical day: lots of driving and lots of walking. We finally knocked off at nine. We would go to Tina's apartment the next day. We both were exhausted.

When I got home, I passed up my vodka for a Sprite. I knew that the vodka might put me out. I called Jimmy to postpone our tentative trip to Connecticut—I wouldn't be able to leave town with the Tina case open. The answering machine blinked four messages. It had been a slow day. Message two was from Molly: "Hi, Danny. Too bad you had to leave dinner. I was really enjoying it. I guess that kind of thing comes up a lot in your line of work. Remember, I get a free dinner every month. Perhaps next time we'll get the chance to finish the meal. Maybe we'll even get to have a grappa with our espresso."

I quickly called her cell.

"Hi," she said.

"It's Danny."

"I was hoping you'd call."

"Well, I was hoping you'd answer." *Jesus, can't you do better than that, Martell?* "I was hoping we could do it again. Soon."

"That sounds great. How soon?"

"If I don't have to work a fourteen-hour day, how about tomorrow?"

"I'm supposed to work, but I think I could get Jenny to take over my shift."

"Let's say I call you at four."

"Sure. Where do you want to go?"

"How about me cooking? I'm not bad. Is there anything you don't eat?"

"No, though I'm not into endangered species."

"That's outside my budget anyway," I said, laughing.

When I hung up, I went to the kitchen. I realized I was whistling. I also knew that I wasn't in the mood for Sprite. I poured myself a generous vodka, and as I took the first hit of it, I smiled. God bless Molly Juste. Why? That was easy. She made me feel good.

We started the next day at seven. We were barely in the apartment an hour when we hit gold. Alex was going through the closets, and I was tossing the living room. There was a battered rolltop desk in the corner. I pulled out the drawers and found some old lipsticks and a bunch of unpaid bills. Then I pushed open the top. Bingo. I picked up a large, expensive leather appointment book. I went to the last page. There, at the right date and time, was the entry: *Vic and Donnie*. I pulled out the list of license plate matches for the three numbers our witness had supplied. There, eleventh on the list, was the name Donald Newman. I had a feeling that this might be our Donnie. Motor Vehicles gave us an address on the west side of town.

Newman lived in a small, neat apartment building that was probably built in the thirties. We walked up to the third floor and rang the bell. A short, round young man with thinning blond hair opened the door.

"Is Donald Newman home?" asked Alex.

"No. He's at work."

"Where's that?"

"Why do you want to know?"

We both flipped open our badges and stepped into the apartment.

"What's your name?" I asked.

"What's this all about?"

"We ask, you answer," said Alex. "Name...please."

Our boy suddenly was a shade or two lighter.

"Victor Warren," he answered, with a voice that was tighter than a fist. Double bingo! We didn't have our Donnie yet, but we had our Vic.

"Are you Donald Newman's roommate?"

"No. He's just a friend. I live on Sabin."

"Do you have a white Tahoe?"

"No. I have a Mini Cooper."

"Why don't you sit down on that couch, Vic," I said. "This might take a while."

It didn't take long before Vic was sobbing like an eleven-year-old who had just broken his new PlayStation.

"I didn't do anything. I didn't touch the freak."

"But you were there?" asked Alex.

He nodded his head.

"Where did it happen?" I asked.

He twisted his head and nodded toward the bedroom.

"And Donnie did it alone?"

"Yes. I just watched."

"Did you help him get the body into the car?"

"No. I just held the door open."

"And when you got to the park?"

"Same thing."

We went on for another fifteen minutes before I signaled to Alex that it was time to take Vic downtown. Vic really started crying when we cuffed him and took him downstairs. I almost felt sorry for him, but not that much. I had been doing this long enough to know that Vic was dirty. He had done a lot more than open doors.

After three hours we got Vic to admit that he had helped carry Tina into Newman's car. There would be a lot more to come, so we put the still-crying Vic into a holding cell until we could work on Donnie Newman. We felt that we had a Murder One on both of them. Vic told us that Donnie worked at a Barnes & Noble bookstore on Hope Street, so, after stopping for a sandwich and a beer, we headed there. I called Molly first to confirm our dinner plans.

"You're going to cook, right?" she asked.

"I told you, I'm not bad."

"Okay, I'm convinced. You're too smart to be bullshitting about this. What time?"

"Nine, okay?"

"Perfect. I switched shifts with Jenny, so I'll be out of here with plenty of time to change. Can I bring anything?"

"If it's not out of your way, pick up some arugula and four or five tomatoes. Make sure they're ripe."

"Will do, Sergeant."

"It's Lieutenant, Ms. Juste. Actually Lieutenant First Class."

"Got it, sir. I'll see you tonight at twenty-one hundred hours."

Donnie was working at the information desk. He appeared to be in his midtwenties, tall, with a long, dark brown ponytail held by a rubber band.

"Can I help you?"

"I think you can," I said, taking out my badge. "Why don't you tell your boss that something's come up, and you have to leave early. Or we can cuff you here and duckwalk you out."

"What's this all about?"

"Cut the shit, Newman. You know why we're here. Your buddy Vic gave it all to us."

"Whatever he told you is not true. He's lying."

I took my cuffs out and placed them on the counter.

"What do you want to do?" I asked.

We walked Donnie Newman back to the manager's office and waited outside for him. When we put him in the backseat of the car with Alex, he asked us if he could smoke. After we stopped laughing, I drove down to the station house.

Newman was a hard case. While Warren didn't have a record, Newman did. He had had an assault rap and a B and E. Both were eventually dismissed. We took turns with him for almost two hours. All we got was "I don't know what the fuck you're talking about." It was strange that a guy like this was working at a book-store. We thought he'd fold quickly. Warren had given us enough to get an easy Murder Two on him, and he had given us a ton on Newman. We started to make progress when we showed him the impression of his sneaker and the partial print from Tina's neck.

"That could be anyone's sneaker," he said.

"It could be, but it isn't," I told him. "These things are as good as fingerprints. We took the sneaker from your apartment. It's an exact match."

"I don't believe it. I keep telling you I don't know what the fuck you're talking about."

The door opened, and Marty Morel came in and handed Alex a folded piece of paper.

"It's a three-point shot at the buzzer. You win the game. It's a perfect match."

We didn't have to ask Marty anything. We had fingerprinted Newman when we brought him in. The lab guys had matched his print against the one that had been lifted from the victim's neck.

"How about this, Mutt?" asked Alex as he opened the paper.

"What the fuck is this?"

"It's the lease for your new apartment in Cranston," I said. "I'd say it's a twenty-five- or maybe even thirty-year lease. Unfortunately, the place is small. Only eight by twelve feet. But it's real cheap. And it's rent controlled."

"If you get lucky, maybe you'll find another Tina to share the place with," Alex added.

"I think I want a lawyer."

"Here's my cell. The call's on me," I said.

We spent another hour with Newman until Ronnie Melman from the DA's office came in and took over. By the time Ronnie arrived, Newman had changed his tune. Yes, he was there, but it was Vic who had killed Tina. They were both going away for a long time, but Newman would do more. After all, the print was his. Case closed.

Captain Kitty was actually smiling when we filled her in.

"I would say nice work, but that wouldn't even touch on it. You've saved this department from getting a ton of heat we didn't need. Frisch was ready to run the story tomorrow. Now it'll be a straight murder in the park. No wings." Alex looked at me and smiled. "I'm going to talk to the chief and put this in your file. It'll come in handy when you strong-arm another mutt. Now go and get a drink on me and take tomorrow off."

"Thanks, Captain," I said.

As we left she called out, "I'll buy you two drinks if you can tell me what *claudicant* means."

"Lame or having a limp, Cap," said Alex. "Thanks to you, I'm hooked on A Word A Day. Hope you don't mind if I order a couple of glasses of champagne. I feel very bubbly today."

CHAPTER TWENTY-EIGHT

I **GOT** home early enough to exercise before heading to Federal Hill to shop. I had worked out in my mind the day before what I'd cook for Molly. We'd start with a rice salad caprese, which was essentially a caprese salad with Arborio rice. I could prepare it beforehand and let it sit for an hour before serving. All I had to do before putting it on the table was add some basil. Then I'd serve chicken breast *valdostana* with braised lentils. For a side, I'd make white beans with rosemary and vinegar. As I was leaving the house, the phone rang. I wasn't going to take it, but I saw it was Jimmy Warden calling.

"Hi, Jimmy."

"That's was nice work that you and Poster Boy did. You made the Captain very happy."

"She made me very happy, too. I have tomorrow off."

"I know. Think you'd still like to take a ride to Connecticut with me? I'm heading up tomorrow. I'm going to talk to the trooper who headed up the investigation into the murders."

I had planned to do some work in the backyard and put my tax info together, but most of all, I wanted to finally take care of Linda's stuff. I had let Linda's mother and sister go through all her clothes and jewelry, keeping what they wanted and giving the remainder to Goodwill. Now I had to deal with all the rest: letters, diaries, photos, the hundreds of things that were jammed into her briefcase, pocketbooks, desk drawers, on and on. Every time I came across a piece of her past, her life, I would stare at it for I couldn't say how long and then numbly walk around the house, trying to figure out what I had intended to do before that.

In the beginning I cried each time. Not big, blubbery sobs, just on-and-off waves of small tears that went on for too long. I hadn't yet been able to sort out my feelings. I still didn't have the guts to really confront where we were when she left. I loved her, but the relationship was like a pennant on a boat that had been whipped by winds too long, more than a bit tattered and faded. And though I didn't have direct proof, I felt she had been having an affair. So far, I hadn't found anything to confirm that. No strange initials in her datebook for lunches or dinners. No names on the cell phone that I didn't know. I had no evidence except my gut, which kept yelling at me that she was screwing someone else. That's not the way a man should think about his late wife.

What I wanted to do but hadn't had the guts to do yet was call Sasha, Linda's best friend, and confront her. I knew exactly what I would say: "I need the truth, Sasha. You won't be betraying anything. Linda is gone. Just tell me simply. Yes or no. Was she having an affair?"

"Where the fuck are you?" asked Jimmy in a loud voice. "Can you make it?"

"Sure, Jimmy."

"Great. I'll pick you up at eight. We have to go to Salisbury. It's in the northwest part of the state."

"See you tomorrow."

That night, Molly showed up exactly on time, which is something I love. In one hand she held a bunch of irises, and in the other, a bottle of wine.

"Reporting for duty, Lieutenant," she said, and she kissed me on both cheeks.

"At ease, Officer," I said, and I kissed her back.

We had a great evening. I could see that Molly loved the food and the wine she brought, a Corvo from Sicily, which was perfectly suited to the meal. Afterward, we went to the living room for coffee and grappa. Molly had told me over dinner that she had a DVD of a scene she had just done in class that she wanted me to see. I put it in the DVD player with trepidation. What if she was lousy? Could I fake liking her work convincingly? The scene was from Arthur Miller's *A View from the Bridge*. Happy surprise: she was terrific. When it was finished, I sat quietly for a moment. It took her a while to ask me what I thought.

"You were good. Really good. But I have a concern."

"Concern?"

"Yes."

"And what's that?"

"That you'll soon be moving to New York or LA, and then I won't be able to see you."

"Do you know what you're saying?"

"No. I only know what I'm thinking."

And then we were kissing. Her lips were fur soft, and her body fit against mine like a piece of a puzzle. Her taste was cool, and her skin smelled like a baby's after a bath. I don't know how long it went on, but then Molly said, pulling away, "This is too good. I don't think we should go further now, even though I want to."

I could barely get out, "Why?"

"Because you need more time. Linda really left you just a moment ago. You've barely started to grieve, Danny. I felt something for you the first time we met, but I pushed my feelings back because I knew you were married."

"Knew?"

"I thought *you* were the detective. Look at your left hand. You're still wearing your wedding band."

I reached out and touched the side of her face.

"When can I see you again? Do I have to wait a year? How will you know that I've sufficiently finished my course of grieving?"

"Why don't I call you next week, and we'll set up another dinner date."

"That sounds great."

I walked her to the door.

"I have one question, Molly."

"What's that?"

"Can I have a good-night kiss?"

CHAPTER TWENTY-NINE

JIMMY WARDEN was an on-time guy. So, at almost precisely eight Friday morning, two blasts of his car horn told me that he was sitting in my driveway. It took me only the time to throw on my jacket and go down the stairs before I was opening the car door.

"You're on time, and you don't look like shit. Congratulations. I think you might make it."

"Coming from you, that's a big compliment. Let's pick up some coffee."

"How about Starbucks?"

"Jesus, Jimmy. I go through this with Alex all the time. I'm Italian, and I need good coffee. Real coffee. Swing by Cicognani's on Federal Hill. Their coffee is great, and the pastries are even better."

After stopping there, Jimmy headed to Route 395. Once on it, he set the cruise control to seventy, five above the speed limit, and we headed toward Hartford.

"Chris Ross is the guy we're going to meet. He was a captain in the state police and headed up the investigation into the killings. He retired last year."

"I wasn't able to read the folder you sent me on them. Why do you think there might be a connection to our piece of business? Didn't these things happen ten years ago?"

"Eleven. They were called the Straw Hat Murders because all the victims were found with what looked like small woven straw caps on their heads. There were four of them—all women."

"How old?"

"From late teens to thirty or so."

We stayed on the Straw Hats for another ten minutes, until Jimmy said that we'd be covering the same ground when we met with Ross, so we switched to the new novel by Michael Connelly that Jimmy had given me the week before. By the time we had chewed that over, we were past Hartford and headed toward Torrington, then west to Salisbury.

Since his retirement, Chris Ross had started a swimming-pool-maintenance business with his brother, Jerry. We met him at their office, in what had been a large garage, located just behind the town hall in Salisbury.

Ross was a tall man who stood taller. He was lean, but you could sense there were muscles to spare under his gray work shirt. He had a crew cut, which figured when you noticed the Corps tattoo on the back of his right hand. He had a smile that was warm and open, but you sensed that he used it sparingly. Chris Ross said that his brother had a customer coming into the office in a few minutes, so it might be better if we talked at the diner down the road.

"I think we won't be overheard here," said Ross, leading us to a booth at the other end of the counter.

"What do you know about our case?" asked Jimmy after we ordered lunch.

"I get the *Globe*, so I've read their coverage on it. It sure reminds me of our piece of business. But that was a long time ago. It still eats away at my ass that we didn't nail the guy. My guess is that he just moved on or died."

"What was the spacing?"

"They were all within two months of each other. Then there was a gap of almost a year. The last one was almost a year and a half after that. And that was it."

"As I remember from the material you sent me, the first two were young."

"Number one was just eighteen. The next one was a week short of her twentieth birthday. That case was a real bitch. She was the niece of one of my men."

Jimmy played with his scrambled eggs for a moment before asking Ross, "Did you ever land any likelies?"

"No. We rolled in everyone that had an assault rap—male or female—on their record. We also looked at everyone who was new to the area. Nothing. These towns are small, quiet places, and people know each other, but we never got anything of use."

"Did you pick up any prints?"

"Not a one. The guy must have used gloves."

"How do you think he took them?"

"The first two were probably looking for a ride. People here don't hitch much, but you see lots of kids walking on the road. Chances are that he just pulled alongside and asked if he could give them a lift. Probably looked harmless. As I said, this is a quiet, safe area. Nothing like that ever happened here. You guys see a world we don't even have a clue about. We have the occasional break-in here, a lot of auto accidents, some fatal, a suicide once in a while, and, every five years or so, a murder-suicide. That's about it."

"The others?" I asked.

"One was a teacher. Preschool. Lived with another woman, who was on vacation at the time. He broke into the house. Probably late. We found the body two days later in the woods about a mile away. The last one lived alone in the village of Kent. We found her car in the parking lot of a restaurant. Our guess was that he grabbed her as she was getting into the car. It took us a week to find her. Also in the woods. About five miles away."

"And the straw hats?" asked Jimmy.

"That was really the odd part. They were all made from the same ornamental grass. Muhlenbergia. Grows all over the place. When it's dry it resembles straw. These 'hats' didn't really look like hats. That all came from the newspapers. I think the *Hartford Courant* came up with it."

"What did they look like?" I asked.

"I'd say they were more like crowns. They had points all around. And a small cross sticking out of the top." I looked over at Jimmy. He was writing something in his black leather notebook. "They were very well made. I mean the weaving, or whatever you'd call it, was carefully done. The guy definitely didn't put them together in the woods at night."

Jimmy waved to the waitress for the bill and said to Ross, "Do you think you have the time to show us a couple of the places where you found them?"

"Sure. One's only a couple miles from here."

Unlike in Providence, there was no shortage of remote, wooded spots to dispose of a body without being spotted. The area was still rural, with a number of working farms, and according to Ross, more than half the roads were dirt. We drove up a steep, winding road with only a few houses, which were set far back from the road.

"It's right here," said Ross, and he pulled over next to a small stream that ran beneath the road. We followed him through thick second-growth woods until he stopped at a large, circular patch of moss. "This is where we found the teacher."

"Did he drag her here?" asked Jimmy.

"There was no sign of that. We think he carried her in. Probably on his shoulders."

"How far is it from the road?"

"We walked it off. A little over four hundred yards."

"Well," said Jimmy, "you certainly weren't looking for a weakling."

Ross drove us to where they found the first victim. He pulled over near a field where some cattle were feeding. They were each black with a thick white band around the middle.

"What are those called?"

"Belted Galloways. A number of farmers here breed them."

This time, we walked through thick underbrush beneath a canopy of pine trees. We'd gone in fewer than a hundred feet when Ross stopped.

"It was right here," he said, standing next to a large oak. "He left her propped up against this tree."

"There were no shoe or boot prints?" I asked.

"Nothing. Ground was hard."

Ross was open to show us the other sites, but since we had a long drive back, we thanked him and left.

We drove for almost an hour without speaking. Then Jimmy spoke.

"I think it's the same guy."

I didn't respond, but I thought he was right.

CHAPTER THIRTY

Two days later the phone woke me up. Early? It was still dark! I looked at the clock on the bedside table. Five fucking forty-four.

"Yes?" I croaked.

"Get over to Pawnee Place." Captain Kitty, of course. "Number thirty-two. It's just off of Granger."

I sat up, more or less awake.

"What's up?" I paused a moment. I could barely get it out. "Another Angel?"

"No. But it's big. Very big. I'm putting everyone on this. I'll tell you when you get there. And call your partner. I want him there, too."

There were nine squad cars and six unmarked when I arrived fifteen minutes later. I spotted the coroner walking out of the building, a small three-story apartment house. Kitty was just behind him.

"What's up?" I asked as I walked over to her.

"I'll meet everyone by the van in five minutes. I'll fill you in then. Meanwhile, get them all together."

It was almost a half hour before Kitty showed up. Only Paul Fierlinger and Donnie Degnan had been up at the crime scene, and they didn't have a chance to fill us in.

"What's going on, Captain?" asked Ted Sammons, a third grade from the Second Division.

"Move in a little more, guys. Let's keep this close. You start, Paul."

"We got a double in the back apartment on the third floor. Man and woman. Real mess. We found a small axe next to the man's body. It looked more like a chain saw was used than an axe. From the time of the nine-one-one call, I'd say we got here maybe fifteen minutes after it happened. So far no one saw the perp, but it's not a job that a woman can do."

"Who caught it?" That was Alex. He was standing right behind me.

"That's what makes this a big, big mess," said Kitty. "The man was Thomas Nardini."

You could almost hear everyone take a deep breath. Nardini was a city councilman who represented Ward Four, North End. A lot of people expected him to run for mayor, and more than that expected him to win. He was also the governor's first cousin.

"The woman with Nardini had a driver's license in her purse. Her name is Jill Perkins. Thirty-two. Lived in Woonsocket. Nardini's married. Our assumption is that Perkins was a 'friend.' The apartment was rented to a Max Loomis. He works in Nardini's office. We haven't been able to locate him yet."

"It sounds like the film I saw last weekend. It's called *The Apartment*. This guy, Jack Lemmon, gives out his apartment to people who want to shack up," said Timmy Jessup, a second grade from our division.

"Skip the damn review, Jessup," barked Kitty. "This is very serious shit. Do you have anything else, Paul?"

"It doesn't look like either one put up a fight. Nardini probably opened the door, and the guy gave it to him. The woman was found in the bathroom. No money was taken."

"Who called?" I asked.

"That's the weirdest part. The nine-one-one call came in on Nardini's cell. We found the phone on the living room floor." He stopped for a moment and looked down at the ground. "The Axe Man made the call."

"I'm telling you now," Kitty broke in, "I never want you to use the 'Axe Man' tag. For the time being, I'm just going to tell the press that they died from a beating. Nothing more." We all nodded. "I'm putting everyone who can walk on this case. Those of you who got pulled out of bed should go home now and shower and have some coffee. Then get right back. The rest of you will be broken into teams, and I want you to work your asses off."

CHAPTER THIRTY-ONE

I PICKED up Alex three hours later and headed for the station. We were told that we'd be teamed up with Phil Lowman and Bev Sheehy. Though we didn't have many female detectives on the force, Bev was one of the best. Smart, tough, and imaginative.

Brad Morse from the Seventh was heading up two of the five teams. He came in and told us we were assigned to go to Woonsocket and check out the woman who was with Nardini. Morse handed us a printout of what had been dug up on Jill Perkins: her home address, where she worked, and a bunch of other things that one would find out from the contents of a person's wallet.

It took us a half hour to cover the twenty miles to Woonsocket. We decided before we left that Alex and I would take the home, and Phil and Bev her office.

Jill Perkins had lived in the back unit on the ground floor of a small Victorian three-story building. First we went to each apartment—there were two on a floor—and knocked on the door. An elderly man lived in the apartment opposite hers. We identified ourselves and told the man that Jill Perkins had been in an accident. That's it—just an accident.

"That's terrible," he said. "I hope she's all right. She's a terrific girl."

We asked him if anything unusual had happened to Ms. Perkins. Fights, arguments, that kind of thing. No, she was a perfect neighbor. Friendly and quiet. There was only one other apartment occupied, on the third floor, and we got the same reaction from the young woman who lived there: Jill Perkins was a perfect neighbor.

Before we left the building, I went alone into Jill Perkins's apartment. Alex had some calls to make, probably either war gaming or his date for that night. The apartment was small but bright. The furniture looked recent, and everything was clean and in place. I quickly found her address book and her answering machine. The light was blinking, and it said there were nine messages. I unplugged it and took it with me.

We split up and worked opposite sides of the street. Nothing. The info sheet showed she belonged to a gym—the Fitness Palace—a few blocks away. The guy at the desk was wearing a skintight T-shirt and looked like he could bench-press the two of us, and the desk.

"Jill? She's a regular. Works out three times a week with Dion and does at least two spinning sessions. She's okay, isn't she?"

We told him she was fine. When you do what we do, it's easy to lie.

"Did she ever have any problems here?" I asked.

"Like what?"

"Arguments. Did anyone bother her? That kind of thing."

"No. She's a sweetheart. Everybody loves her."

I called Alex. They had turned up a big nada, too. So we arranged to meet at Gian Carlo's for lunch. I had eaten there once. Not up to our restaurants on Federal Hill, but pretty good.

Though we were working, we all ordered a drink. Alex and Bev had Bloody Marys, and Phil and I each had a glass of pinot grigio.

"Absolutely nothing?" I asked as we looked at the menu.

"A few bits," said Alex.

"She was married. Short time," said Lowman. "Guy was career military. He's in Afghanistan now. The insurance company she works for says she's a great employee and everyone likes her."

"Anyone talk to her family?" I asked.

"Don't know yet. Probably Kitty. They live in Pittsburgh," said Bev.

"Any siblings?" asked Alex.

"A sister. Lives in New Mexico."

"We have to find her friends."

"We printed out a phone list from her computer. We'll all start banging away after lunch," said Alex.

The afternoon brought more of the same. Nothing. A couple of the people we contacted started crying as soon as we identified ourselves—the Nardini murders were now all over the media. Tomorrow it would be front-page news throughout New England.

We knocked off at seven and drove back. At eight thirty we all went into the rec room to get the wrap-up from Kitty. There had to be forty of us, including Jimmy Warden and a couple of other retired guys. Kitty was really calling in all hands.

"Everybody here?" she asked.

"We're only missing Loper. His wife's in labor!" Brad Morse shouted out.

"Okay. Here's where we're at: The target was definitely Nardini. The woman, Perkins, unfortunately for her, just happened to be there. Here's the story, and some of you might remember it. A little over two years ago, Nardini was backing his car out of his driveway. He hit an eleven-year-old kid on a skateboard. The kid went under the wheels and died on the spot. An accident. Pure and simple."

"The Niccolini kid," I said out loud.

"You got it, Danny. Angelo Niccolini's son."

Angelo Niccolini was head of the Providence mob. He was called Mr. Dirt, for all the people he had put away. Aside from some small time he did as a kid, we had never been able to lay a glove on him.

"We know that Niccolini wanted to kill Nardini on the spot. But he was smart enough to wait. He's also smart enough to have a great alibi. We went to his home, which is on the same block as Nardini's, and found out that he's in Las Vegas. Been there for a week."

"Kitty," said Jimmy, "I'll bet all our IRAs that this was done by outside talent."

"I'm sure you're right, Jimmy. What we have to do is put maximum pressure on every damn wise guy in town. Danny and Tony, you'll head this up. We'll start tomorrow morning. Early. Any questions?"

"Have you called the FBI? I'm sure they have some stuff that we don't."

"You're right, Jimmy. And I already have. Okay. I'll see everyone tomorrow morning. Early."

CHAPTER THIRTY-TWO

Before I went to bed, I called Molly. No answer. I left a message on her machine at home: "Molly, we've got a big one on our plate. Lots and lots of hours until we reel it in. So what does that mean? It means I can't set a time when I can see you, but what I want to tell you is that I really want to see you. Does that make sense? So, until then, I'm thinking of you. A lot."

The other three headed for Woonsocket at eight the next morning. I headed over to Federal Hill. I met Tony LaMarco at Di Blasi's, a sandwich joint that served great espresso. Tony joined the force a year ahead of me. I knew him in high school, where he quarterbacked the team to the state championship. I was a strong safety who mainly sat on the bench. He was a big, easygoing guy with a great sense of humor. And, best of all, he still lived on Federal Hill.

"You really think it was Niccolini?" I asked after finishing a biscotto.

"No question about it. I'm surprised he didn't do it a year ago. What I heard from our guys who got there first, it took four of his guys to keep him from taking Nardini out, right there on the street. But how the hell do we nail him? I'm sure the guy who did the business is from out of town. But from where? LA? Brooklyn?"

"Aside from his number one, Little Augie Fauci, is there anyone else he'd use to set it up?"

"Maybe Billy Dee."

"I thought he died."

"Seventeen years in Leavenworth and two different kinds of cancer, and he's still around. He'll wind up burying both of us."

"Does he still own the dry cleaner down on Claremont?"

"Yeah. His sister runs it, but he hangs out in an office in the back."

"Why don't I see him, and you pay a call on Little Augie. That list we drew up last night is where we should have the rest of the crew work."

"I don't think they'll get much. None of the soldiers know anything."

"I agree, but that's what Kitty wants."

"Where do you want to have lunch?"

"How about my uncle's place? Say, one thirty?"

Billy Dee wasn't at the dry cleaner, but I found him at the Two Roses Social Club around the block. He was reading the *Globe* and having his shoes shined. The other wise guys were playing casino at a table in the back.

"I have to talk to you, Billy."

"I don't know a fucking thing, Martell," he answered in a voice that sounded as if someone were pressing down on his windpipe.

"You don't even know what I want to talk about," I said.

"Who the fuck are you kidding?" He tossed a ten-dollar bill to the kid who shined his shoes, and stood up. Billy was probably five five when he was first arrested, forty years ago, and now was closer to five three. I don't know if he worked out, but he looked strong. Even if you didn't know who he was and what he had done, you still wouldn't want to mess with this little old guy.

"When does Joe Dirt get back from Vegas?" I asked.

"Joe who?"

"Angelo Niccolini, Billy. Your boss."

"I don't have a boss. I own my own business."

"That's right. I forgot. You're an entrepreneur. You're the backbone of this country, Billy."

"Unless you have a warrant, Martell, get the fuck out of here. This is a private social club, and you're not a member."

"Let me tell you something, Billy. We're going to be all over you and your crew until we find Nardini's killer. Make sure you tell Angelo that."

"Tell him yourself, Martell."

I leaned on Billy Dee for another five minutes before I split. As I was walking back to my car, my cell phone rang. It was Captain Kitty.

"Our guys who've been watching Angelo Niccolini's house say that he just got home from Vegas. Pick up LaMarco and head over to his place."

Angelo Niccolini lived in a huge three-story brick house that sat in the middle of the block. Painted a dark brown that was almost black, it was easily the largest on the street and seemed more like a part of the Maginot Line than a family home. Nardini's house, a small Cape, was four houses down from it.

Tony and I walked up the front steps and rang the bell. A short, overweight woman in tight jeans opened the door. It was Niccolini's wife, Patti.

"Hello, Mrs. Niccolini. I'm Detective LaMarco, and this is Detective Martell," Tony said as we both showed our IDs.

"Angelo's sleeping," she said. She started to close the door. I put my hand out and stopped her.

"Wake him up. We have to see him."

"He just got in from Vegas. Come back later."

"We have to see him now," said Tony. "Right now."

"Do you have a warrant?"

"If we have to get a warrant," I said, "we'll keep him for a minimum of forty-eight hours, no matter how good his lawyer is. I don't think he'd like that."

"Fucking cops. You never leave him alone." She turned and went back into the house. A few minutes later, Niccolini came out.

"Hi, Angelo," I said. Like his house, Niccolini was big. An easy 250, with arms that looked more like thighs.

"What can I do for you and LaMarco?"

"We want to talk about the Nardini murder."

"All I know is what I read in the papers. I was in Vegas when it happened."

"Yeah, we heard," said Tony.

"I guess I should say I'm sorry, but I'm not. That miserable piece of shit killed my son, Angelo Junior. I hope he rots in hell."

"When was the last time you went out of town?"

"I go to Vegas a couple of times a year. I used to go more when Siegfried and Roy were doing their show. That tiger thing was a tragedy. I loved them."

"You're not going to beat this, Angelo. We're going to find the punk you hired," Tony said.

"Lots of luck, LaMarco. You won't lay a glove on me. Nardini had lots of enemies. When he bought it, I was playing blackjack. I even won a couple of thou."

"We have a lot to talk to you about, Angelo. Are you going to invite us in?"

"I don't think so. I'm allergic to fuzz. But I'll tell you what I'll do. I'll come down and see you later today with my lawyer. Say, four o'clock. How does that sound?"

Tony and I looked at each other. We were not going to do it, but we both wanted to beat the shit out of this creep. We just turned and walked down to our car.

CHAPTER THIRTY-THREE

IT WAS no surprise when Angelo Niccolini walked into Captain Kitty's office with Ira Wingate III. Wingate was the town's top criminal lawyer and had represented all of Angelo's crew since he got out of law school. His father, Ira Wingate II, had stopped practicing a few years back, when he was convicted with jury tampering. He did just under ten months at the Donald Price Medium Security Facility and was now living most of the year in Boca.

None of us disliked Wingate because he represented mutts. After all, everyone's entitled to a lawyer. What we couldn't stand was that he saw himself as a junior wise guy. Ira was five five and at least forty pounds overweight, but his expensive tailored suits disguised at least twenty pounds of it. There were three photos of him in Scalise's restaurant on Federal Hill. Scalise's was the favorite hangout for the "boys."

"Captain, I hope this won't take much time. I have to meet a couple of clients in a half hour."

"Mr. Wingate, this will take as long as it takes. We're investigating the brutal murder of two good people. And we believe that your client knows quite a lot about it."

"Mr. Niccolini was three thousand miles away when this terrible attack occurred."

"We know that. We also know that he threatened Mr. Nardini's life."

"In a moment of grief, he might have said some things that any normal person would say. I'm sure you can understand that."

"What I want you to understand, Mr. Wingate, is that we will not stop until we find the persons involved in this. Notice that I said *persons*. This was a murder for hire. I'm throwing everything we have at this."

Just then, the phone rang. Captain Kitty's cat Cuffs, who had been sleeping, jumped from her bookcase to the floor.

"Yes," she said into the phone. "What? Okay, I'll be right out." She stood up and walked to the door. She motioned for Tony and me to follow. "Mr. Wingate, we'll be back in a few minutes."

"Remember, Captain, I have a meet—"

We followed Kitty to Phil Larson's office. Phil ran three precincts and was Kitty's boss.

"What's up? We had Niccolini in my office."

"I know. You can let him and that piece of shit Wingate go."

"Why? We just started, Phil."

"We found the killer. His name is Benji Filicia. A hitter from Phoenix. He was found floating in the bay. Capped twice in the back of the head. His thumbprint matches the one found at the scene. I'm sure Niccolini cleared the hit with the Parma brothers, who run the Arizona mob. We'll never get to him now."

"We still haven't gotten through all the phone records," I said.

"Danny, without the perp we're nowhere. Unless one of the boys opens up, and I doubt that will happen, we're at a dead end."

"What about having our friends in Phoenix put the squeeze on the Parmas?"

"I have a call in to them, Kitty. I think they'll be as successful as we were up here."

"Is it okay if I keep Danny and Tony on this for another week or so?"

"Sure. But you're dreaming if you think one of his boys will give you anything."

"Ralphie Bonducci is going to be sentenced in a month," said Tony. "He's looking at an easy ten to twelve. If we can promise that we'll try to get him five max, maybe that will refresh his memory about the Nardini hit."

"Why not. Give it a shot, Tony."

We went back to Kitty's office. When I opened the door, Angelo was doing the sudoku from the paper. Wingate was on his cell phone.

"I'm still waiting on that check, Sal. If you want me at your hearing, you'd better get it in. Like, today."

"You both can leave, Mr. Wingate," said Kitty.

"We're finished so soon? I delayed my meeting," said Wingate, smiling.

"Get out of here. Both of you," said Kitty in a voice approach-ing a snarl. "And don't think for a moment we're finished with you, Mr. Niccolini. We have a lot of leads and phone calls to go through."

"Sure you do. I'm real worried. Cops in skirts always scare me."

"Shut up, punk," said Tony.

"Relax, LaMarco. You know, I really want you to catch the guy. And when you do, I'll pin a medal on him," said Niccolini, laughing.

CHAPTER THIRTY-FOUR

FOR THE first time in quite a while, I got home at a reasonable hour, six thirty. I went downstairs to the gym and worked out for almost an hour. I called Molly at home, but all I got was her machine. I left a message for her to call me later. I said that I was free for dinner. After showering I went downstairs, poured myself a beer, and started to go through a dozen magazines that had piled up in the past few weeks. The only one I spent time on was *The Economist*. I had been hooked on it since I'd gotten it as a Christmas gift when I was in law school. There was a terrific obit on an Indian politician I had never heard of.

I was heading into the kitchen to get another beer, when the front doorbell rang. It took me a moment to take in the very attractive woman standing there.

"Hi, Danny."

Her hair was different—pixie cut and dyed blond, very blond. She seemed taller; then I noticed she was wearing high, high heels. She had on a short gray skirt with a long-sleeved silk shirt. It was my old girlfriend Sally Falcone, and she looked great. *Girlfriend* was not really accurate, though, since we had been engaged for almost a year.

"Sally! Come on in," I said as I led her into the living room.

After I brought her a Pellegrino, we sat down on the big leather couch.

"I heard about your wife, Danny. I'm really sorry."

I tried to say something but couldn't. She reached out and touched my hand. Then I pulled it together.

"I thought you lived in Seattle," I said in a voice that sounded far away.

"I moved back here last month. Allan and I are getting divorced."

"I'm sorry to hear that."

"Well, I'm not. The last two years have been hell."

"Are you going to stay in Providence?"

"I'd better. I took a job with McGrath and Weinberg. And I bought a condo."

"Boy, you move fast."

Just then, the phone rang. I had a feeling it was Molly, so I took it in the kitchen.

"Danny?"

"Hey, that's a voice I haven't heard recently. Two questions: Is everything okay? And are you free for dinner tonight?"

"Yes and yes."

"I'll pick you up at nine, and if you have some vodka, please put it in the freezer for me."

"Why?"

"For our next dinner."

"Absolutely, sir. And the vodka also happens to be Absolut."

I went back to the living room. Sally was looking at a book that she had taken from a pile on the coffee table.

"I heard that this is good."

It was a novel by Margaret Atwood. I think it was the last book that Linda had bought.

"I can't say. I haven't read it."

"Would you mind if I borrowed it?"

I wanted to say no. Because if Sally took the book, she'd have to return it. And that would probably lead to her inviting me to have dinner at her condo. And as good a woman as I knew Sally to be, the woman I wanted in my life was Molly. I hadn't admitted that to myself before. But now that I had, I knew it was right. And it made me feel very good.

CHAPTER THIRTY-FIVE

THAT NIGHT I took Molly to Martelli's. I introduced her to my uncle, who immediately brought over a bottle of Barolo. A few minutes after he left, my grandmother came to the table. She was there not to see me but to give Molly the once-over. I could see she approved. After a quick consultation with Molly, I ordered veal piccata *limone* and chicory-and-arugula salad. Most of the other diners were gone from the restaurant when I ordered *panna cotta* for our dessert.

My uncle brought over a bottle of grappa. I hadn't seen him since we came in, and I knew that he and my grandmother were burning up the family lines giving them a heads-up on Molly. As we finished up, she said that next time we'd have dinner at her place, and she'd do the cooking. And that would be on Saturday, four days away. I was feeling no pain when I drove her home.

"Don't forget we have a date on Saturday," she said when I stopped in front of her building. Then she leaned over and kissed me. The touch of her full, soft lips was warm and light. And she was the one who put her hand behind my neck and pulled me toward her. After I watched her walk into her building, I just sat there for a long time. How long? I have no idea.

Tony picked me up at nine the next morning. Our first and only stop was to see Ralphie Bonducci. Ralphie, whose brother Florio, like Benji Filicia, was also found in the bay three years ago (minus his head), lived on the other side of the river on Point Street. Tony had called him after we left Kitty's office.

Since we knew he wouldn't want to be seen with us, we arranged to meet him at a diner halfway between the city and Barrington.

The place was called Over Easy. We found Ralphie in a booth in the back. After we both ordered coffee, Tony started right in.

"I told you on the phone we can do something big for you, Ralphie. Cut your time in half. Maybe more. But we need something big in exchange."

"I got it. I can give you the shooter in the hotel robbery case three months ago."

"We need something a lot bigger than that," I said.

"What do you mean?"

"Nardini," said Tony. "We know that your boss ordered the hit."

"I don't know a fucking thing about it."

"We don't need you to testify," I said. "No one will ever know. Just tell us who he used to set up the hit."

"I'm not saying I could, but if I did, I'd need more than a half-ass promise that you'd talk to the DA."

"We're meeting him this afternoon, Ralphie. We'll get it for you in writing."

The next day, after setting up a meeting between Irv Biderman, the DA, and Ralphie, we met him again at the diner. This time he had something for us. And it was pure gold.

"You'll never get a thing by checking Angelo's phone action or fax or anything like that. Angelo didn't go to college, but he's smart. What I heard was that Billy Dee set it up for Angelo. And don't bother checking his phone, either. When it's important, he goes to his sister's place in Warwick. That's the phone he used. It was Billy Dee and Angelo. No one else was in on it. But you have a problem."

"What's that?" asked Tony.

"You won't get anything out of Billy Dee. You could put his balls in a Cuisinart, and all he'd do is smile. There's no one tougher."

When we got back, we went straight up to Kitty's office. We kicked around what Ralphie had given us. We all agreed that he was probably right. Even a Murder One indictment wouldn't open Billy Dee up. After a few minutes, Kitty snapped her fingers.

"I got it."

"We're listening," I said.

"What's his sister's name?"

"Angela, I think," said Tony.

"You two weren't on the force when Billy Dee went up on his fed drug rap, but his sister was there every day of his trial. They're fraternal twins. He cares about her more than he does his wife."

"So?"

"We push to get her indicted."

"For what?" Tony asked.

"For being a party to the killing of Nardini. The call was made from her house. He'll do anything to keep her out of this."

"It seems like a mighty long shot to get her indicted," I said.

"You're right, Danny. All we have to do is make Billy Dee believe that we might get it. He'll be a different guy as soon as he hears that we're bringing her in front of the grand jury."

We went to see Billy Dee the next day. He was just back from Atlantic City. Like his boss, he loved to gamble, but unlike him, he didn't like to fly. So when he wanted to shoot craps, he drove to Atlantic City.

This time we found Billy Dee at his dry-cleaning store. His office in back of the store had a beat-up desk, two metal folding chairs, a wide-screen TV, and a Boston Red Sox banner hanging limply on the wall.

"Don't you guys ever give up?"

He was watching *The Dr. Oz Show*. We let him keep it on because the sound was off.

"We traced a call to the Parma brothers in Phoenix to you, Billy."

"That's bullshit, Danny Boy. I never called them from my place or on my cell."

"He didn't say you made the call from there, Billy," said Tony.

"Then what the fuck are you talking about?"

"We're talking about the call you made from Warwick. The one from your sister Angela's house. Does that refresh your memory?"

"That's bullshit," he said as his face flushed.

"We're going to lay our cards on the table," I said. "I doubt if we can nail you on the setup. But we sure as shit can get your sister in front of a grand jury."

"She hasn't done anything!" he shouted.

"Too fucking bad," said Tony.

"She just had a new valve put in her heart."

"Well," I said, "the pressure of going before the grand jury will be a good test for it."

"You miserable motherfuckers. I'll get you both for this. I swear I will."

"Are you threatening us, Billy? You're a two-strike guy—that could buy you a bunch of trouble."

"Why don't you think it over. I think there's a way to work this out," I said.

As we walked out, we heard a crash from Billy's office.

"Who do you think that was, Danny? The desk or the chair?"

We were still laughing when we ordered *macchiatos* around the corner at Loretto's Espresso Bar.

CHAPTER THIRTY-SIX

WHEN I got home that night, there was a message on the machine from Molly: "I hope my favorite detective won't be angry with me, but I have to change our plans for tomorrow night. I can still make dinner with you—nothing could stop that!—but I can't actually make dinner. You're probably thinking that I've been bluffing about my cooking skills. I might not be as good as you, but one day soon you'll see that I really have some ability. Why I can't have you over on Saturday is because of the play I was in as an understudy—as of two this afternoon, I now have the role. Sandy, a friend of mine who was playing the daughter, came down with—if you can believe it—the mumps. It's a pretty good part. So...I have some real work ahead of me. The play opens in one week. I thought maybe you could pick me up at the theater. We're at Theroux Hall on the Brown campus. It's the building next to the library. I'll be finishing up around eight thirty or so. And I heard about a new restaurant—French—that just opened not far from Al Forno. Our chef has been there twice and really likes it. That's a pretty good endorsement. See you tomorrow."

The next day was my chore day: laundry, dry cleaning, food shopping (mainly OJ and fruit), and then lunch at my folks' house. Saturdays now were not much different for me from how they were when Linda was alive. You see, Linda didn't have a strong housekeeping gene. Most Saturdays she was either working in her office or at home. My brother and his girlfriend—now fiancée—were also showing up. I liked her a lot and thought she was perfect for him. They had decided on a date (just four months away), and I was going to be the best man.

Theroux Hall was one of two buildings on the campus that housed a theater. The larger one, Trillin, was where the college drama department put on big Shakespearean productions and musicals. Theroux was used for edgier and more esoteric plays. When I got there, the cast was seated in a circle onstage. I couldn't hear what was being said, but I assumed the man standing in the center was the director. After ten or fifteen minutes, the group broke up, and I went over to the stage and found Molly.

"How's it going?"

"It'll be better if I have a drink."

"Since you know the way to this place, you lead the way. My car's parked on Benefit."

"Illegally, I trust."

"As my father used to tell me all the time, that's the only reason to be a cop."

As we walked to the back of the theater, I spotted someone I knew. *Come on, Martell, what's his name? Of course—he's the guy from the church outreach center. Unusual first name. WASPy. Very. Got it. Brooks…Brooks Shelby.* We walked though the open doors together.

"I didn't know you acted, Mr. Shelby," I said.

He looked at me and smiled.

"You got my name right, but I don't think I know you."

Then I felt a hand on my shoulder. I turned and there was… the other Brooks Shelby.

"Hi, Detective Martell. What brings you here? We don't open for another two weeks." I guess I might have had my mouth open for more than a bit. "Oh, I see you haven't met my brother. My twin brother. Fraternal. Miles, this is Detective Martell." He reached out and shook my hand. His grip was beyond firm.

"Nice to meet you, Detective."

"It's Danny."

"Miles, I think I told you about the detective. He's investigating those terrible killings of the prostitutes. The papers call them the Angel Murders."

Though they looked alike, Brooks Shelby's twin brother was bigger. A lot bigger. They were the same height, but he looked like he had worked out all his life. His chest strained against the buttons of his jacket, and I knew there was no way I could get my hands around his neck.

"Molly," I said as she moved to my side, "why didn't you tell me that the Shelby brothers were acting with you in this production?"

"Your friend is very talented," said Brooks. "I just do the costumes and makeup. My brother, Miles, is the actor."

"We're going out to dinner. Would you two like to join us?" asked Molly.

I was happy to hear them say that they were meeting some friends. I didn't want to share Molly with anybody.

The restaurant, Roquecourbe, really was good, and after an excellent bottle of Burgundy, we wound up closing the place.

"Any chance you might come back to my place?" I asked. "I know I don't want this to end."

"Neither do I."

"So that means yes?"

"It means yes next time. I've got an early class tomorrow, and then I'm working lunch and dinner."

"And when is next time?"

"I have rehearsals every day next week, except Saturday. So that's when it will have to be. Is that okay?"

"Will we be dining at your place?"

"I'm already planning the menu."

CHAPTER THIRTY-SEVEN

BILLY DEE came in to see us on Monday morning. He had on sunglasses and a Red Sox cap pulled down to his nose. We had him wait in an empty office two down from Kitty's. We let him cool for twenty minutes before bringing him into Kitty's office. Inspector Larson was there, too.

"Okay, Billy," I said, "what have you got for us? Whatever it is, we need it now. Right now. The grand jury is sitting down on Wednesday."

"I'll give it to you, but I want it in writing that you'll leave my sister alone."

"I dictated this and had the inspector sign it, too," Kitty said as she handed the sheet of paper to Billy Dee. "It guarantees that your sister won't come up before the grand jury, and her name will be excluded from any court proceedings."

Billy took off his sunglasses and read the note. Either he was a slow reader or he reread it three or four times, because it took five minutes before he placed it down on Kitty's desk.

"I need a couple of things."

"Like what?" asked Larson.

"I'm an older guy. I can't do time."

"You were a participant in the murder of two people. You don't get three months of community service for that."

"All I did was call Aldo Parma and tell him that Angelo wanted a favor. That was it. Parma sent the hitter here. I never met him. It was between Angelo and Parma's guy."

"Can you prove it?" asked Tony.

"They met at the airport when Angelo was getting ready to fly to Vegas."

"Who saw them together?"

"Me."

"And you're prepared to testify to that in court?" Larson asked.

Billy Dee nodded. He suddenly looked a lot older. Larson got up and walked to the door.

"I'm going to call Biderman. I want him to prepare Nardini's indictment."

"There's another thing," said Billy Dee just as Larson opened the door. "I need the witness protection program."

"That's federal. We'll ask. I can't guarantee anything, but I think there's a good chance you'll get in."

"One more thing. I don't care where they put me as long as I can get some decent prosciutto."

About an hour later, Kitty called me.

"You got a minute?"

"Sure."

"I'm leaving. I have to go to Watch Hill. My sister's in the hospital."

"I hope it's not serious."

"No. Just Botox gone wrong. Meet me at my car in the lot."

Kitty was standing next to her car, a new Prius. Kitty was a very green captain. Tony LaMarco was there, too.

"I won't be back for a week, and I wanted to talk to you guys before I left. I'm headed to Northampton for a Scrabble tournament after I see my sister." She handed each of us an envelope. "Read it later. It's a letter from me to the commissioner, and it's cosigned by Larson. See you guys when I get back."

"There was something I wanted to talk to you about, Cap."

"Call me on my cell, Danny."

And that was it. We opened the envelopes. We were both smiling when we finished. Kitty was putting us in for promotions. A real bump and even a better salary uptick.

"You know something, Danny," said Tony as we walked back into the station house, "sometimes I really like this job. Not only does putting that slime bucket away feel good, it's important. We might not be doing God's work, but we're doing something that's right."

CHAPTER THIRTY-EIGHT

ROGER WILLIAMS *Park was deserted. Even though it was after four in the morning, he had waited and watched in his car for thirty minutes before entering the park.*

The Angel was wrapped in her wings. He carried her on his shoulders. With each step, he made a metallic click. Why? He was wearing climbing spikes. Before he reached the tree he had picked out—a huge black oak—he put the Angel down. He quickly climbed, hand over hand, a light pole at the park's entrance. Once at the top, he easily pulled off the security camera.

Fortunately he had noticed it a week before when he checked out the park. With the Angel back on his shoulders, he walked to the oak and started climbing. He smiled as he thought that he was giving this lovely Angel what she deserved—a beautiful view.

CHAPTER THIRTY-NINE

I CALLED Kitty later that afternoon.

"How's your sister?"

"She'll be fine."

"That's great."

"You didn't call me for an update on my sister's botched Botox. What's on your mind, Danny?"

"We've almost wrapped up the Nardini case. Alex is off working on those liquor-store holdups on the East Side. They have some good photos of the crew who did the jobs from the camera in the last store. He feels that they'll be rounding them up today or tomorrow."

"Yeah, I know."

"Well, Alex and I want to get back to the Angels."

"Do you have any new leads?"

"No."

"Let me think about it."

"This is important to me."

"I know, Danny. We'll talk about it when I get back."

I knocked off early and headed straight to Jimmy Warden's. I knew if I went home I'd have a quick vodka and then another one. And then switch to white wine and wind up sleeping on the living room couch.

It took only a minute or so after Jimmy opened the door for him to say, "Okay. What's the fucking problem?"

I asked for a vodka, and he said, "Too early. We'll both have a beer." I followed him into the kitchen, where we sat down at the table. "Did I tell you I'm going out with someone you know?"

"No. Who?"

"Dolores Ricci."

"My father's secretary?" He nodded. "She's very nice. And attractive. Her husband—"

"Was killed in a crash. I-95. The fucker who piled into him was drunk. He's in Moran. Piece of shit gets out in three years."

"How'd you meet?'

"The WW grapevine."

"The WW grapevine?"

"Widows and widowers. It's mainly the women who run it. If they hear of a widower who can fog a mirror, they're all over him. Her best friend, Cindy Rowley, went to school with my wife. She's been trying for over a year to get me to meet Dolores. I wasn't ready until just recently. I'm really glad she did the deed. I hear there's someone you're spending some time with."

"Where'd you hear that?"

"Shmuck, who do you think? After the Red Sox, all your father talks about is you."

"My father's gone from treating me as if I should be living in Guantánamo to being my long-lost brother. He's transferred his feelings for Linda to me."

"Okay. Enough of this relationship crap. What's the problem?"

I told him about my talk with Kitty and wanting to get back on the Angel case.

"Give her a little time. I'm pretty sure she'll put you back on it."

"If she doesn't, would you talk to her?"

"Of course. Now, what else is there?"

"I haven't talked to anyone about this. I've been thinking about leaving the force. I'm not there yet, but I'm thinking."

"In a way, I'm not surprised. When you lose someone like Linda, it turns a lot of things upside down. And when it happens in a sudden and violent way, it throws everything into places you've never seen before. If you leave, what will you do?"

"I'm still a lawyer. I even passed the bar."

"You'd go in with your father?"

"Jesus, no. That would never work."

"Then what?"

"I could set up something on my own, I guess."

"I don't think you've thought this out very much."

And then I started crying. The real thing. Tears big enough to reach for the windshield wipers. Sobbing like a kid whose puppy had been run over. Jimmy, I now realized, was behind me, patting me on the back. A moment later he handed me a vodka.

"I was wrong. You need this." It was a medium-size tumbler. I finished it in two swallows. "Do you need another?"

"I don't think so."

We didn't speak for a few minutes. Maybe more.

"At the end, your relationship with Linda was good, wasn't it?" All I could do was nod. "That's probably part of what you're going through now. I'm not a shrink, but I know this whole thing is going to take some time. And you're lucky to have met this lady. Her name is Molly, right? It shows you're on the right path. She can only help you." Jimmy went and got two more beers. "I'm going to talk to Kitty and see if she'll let me do some work on the Angel. You'll be better when we nail this wack. And keep this stuff about leaving the force to yourself. It's too early. You have a lot of work to do first."

CHAPTER FORTY

I HUNG around Jimmy's until it got dark. Jimmy wanted me to have dinner with him and Dolores and then catch a movie. I told him I didn't think I was up to it.

"You sure?"

"Yeah. I want to pay some bills and finally finish this novel I've been humping at for the last month."

"Stay away from booze, Danny. You had enough here."

"Aye, aye, Captain."

I decided on the way home that I'd eat in. I hadn't cooked in a long time, and I really missed it. I stopped at Pellegrino's and bought a couple of pounds of fennel sausage. I then picked up some plum and heirloom tomatoes (twice the size of my fist) for salad, and broccoli rabe that I'd cook together with the sausages. A simple meal that I knew was just what I needed. Molly couldn't make it because of rehearsals, but she said she'd try to drop over later for a glass of wine.

I didn't start cooking until almost nine. I wanted to start at eight, but I got calls from my mother (two), and my father, my brother, Molly (she was on a break), and Jimmy (did I want to meet them for coffee after the movie?). The sausages were browning nicely when the phone rang again.

"Danny?"

"Yes."

"It's Larson."

The inspector. He had never called me at the house before.

"What's up?"

"We've got a problem. A big one."

"What is it?"

"Another Angel. And this one is really something. The papers and the TV will really flip out for this one."

"Where?"

"Roger Williams Park."

"I'm on my way."

The park was small, with soft lights set under tall elms, and maples that bordered the brick walkways. The two main entrances were blocked by patrol cars. I found Larson with Hughes, Miley, and a couple of guys from the Seventh. The park was located in their precinct. Alex showed up a few minutes later.

"Kitty's on her way from Massachusetts. She'll be here in an hour or so."

"Where's the body?" asked Hughes.

"Is that lift set up?" he called out to someone behind him.

"Ready to go, Inspector."

"Follow me, boys," he said as he started to walk into the park.

We walked toward the Betsy Williams Cottage, which dated from the late eighteenth century. The cottage was near the Elmwood Gate, also blocked off by a squad car. We stopped a hundred feet behind the building, where a lift used by people who work on power lines stood at the base of a large oak tree. We all stepped onto it.

It started up with a jerk. Edwards held a flashlight. At thirty feet we saw it.

"Jesus," muttered Hughes.

This Angel, a white woman in her twenties, was dressed the same as the others, but there was one big difference: she was tied with thick cord, arms spread out, Christlike, to a large branch. I stared at the woman. She didn't look anything like Linda, but that's who I saw. I wanted to touch her, to tell her all the bad stuff was now behind her. But then Alex's voice pulled me out of it.

"How the hell did he do it?" asked Alex.

"That's what we have to find out," said Larson. "At first light I'm having the forensic people look at every inch of the tree and the ground around it. Did he climb up with spikes? Did he use a rope? This woman is slender, but she still has to weigh one-ten. That's not like carrying up a box of chocolates. This thing keeps getting weirder and weirder," he said, holding the flashlight on the woman's face, made up as if she were about to go out on a date.

CHAPTER FORTY-ONE

I DIDN'T get home until almost one. There were three messages on the machine. One was from Molly: "Albert, our director, has a sore throat. Yippee! No rehearsal tomorrow night. Dinner?" One from Kitty: "I'm back. Been to the scene. We're going to meet at nine thirty in my office. Prepare for a long day." The last was from Jimmy Warden: "Spoke to Kitty. I'll be at the meeting in her office tomorrow morning."

Kitty's office was packed. I stood off to the side with Alex and Jimmy. The inspector spoke first.

"The forensic guys finished up an hour ago. Our boy went up the tree wearing spikes. The kind that only serious climbers use. There was no sign that he winched the body up the tree." Three arms shot up. "Let me finish; then I'll take questions. This probably took place the night before. Why wasn't it spotted earlier? Probably because the park doesn't get a lot of traffic, and most people don't look up that high. The victim was killed the same way the others were. Makeup, wings, et cetera, all the same. And yes, she had been picked up four times for prostitution. One here and three in Worcester. She had gone to the outreach program once. We haven't been able to talk to the volunteers yet. Okay, I'll take questions. Yes, Earl."

Earl Winston was from the Fourth. He was a heavy guy who was always going on and off the dreaded weight list.

"Are you saying that this guy climbed the tree with the victim over his shoulder?"

"That's the way it looks."

A chorus of "Jesus," "holy shit," and "wow" rippled across the room.

"We're talking about Mighty Joe Young here," Alex whispered to me.

"Any other questions?"

"I noticed," said Jimmy, "some surveillance cameras around the park. Did they pick up anything?"

"Good question, Jimmy. They picked up nothing. But the camera pointed on the entrance leading directly to the body had been pulled off its mounting. The person who did that climbed up the light stanchion from behind where it was pointing. We found that camera in some bushes near the walkway. And now I'm turning this over to the Captain."

Kitty, who was seated behind her desk, stood up.

"I want you all to know that everything you've been working on has to take a step back. A big step back. A friend at the *Journal* sent this over to me by messenger. It will be in their next edition." She held up the front page of the paper. There, across six of the eight columns, was the picture of the Angel. In color. "The paper was called about the body thirty-seven minutes before we were. We have his voice on tape, but it's obviously muffled. No help there. I want to pull in all known sex offenders again. I'm asking all the other towns in the state to do the same thing. I'm going to put two female officers in disguise on the streets. I've asked the coroner, who's doing the autopsy now, to look again for any sleep-inducing substances."

"Is anyone checking stores that sell tree-climbing footwear?" asked Alex.

"Not yet, Alex, but we certainly will. And, by the way, the victim's name is Gayle Morse. Twenty-two. From Weybridge. Up until four years ago, she was a straight-A student and a promising distance runner at BU. Then she got hooked on crack. Sad story with a sadder end."

CHAPTER FORTY-TWO

Dinner last night with Molly was good. It was her idea to eat out, and I quickly agreed with her. I met Tony LaMarco in the morning at the courthouse for Angelo Niccolini's indictment. There's no better way to kick off a day than by seeing a mutt get indicted. Judge Paul Scherer was on the bench. We all loved Scherer because he disliked mutts as much as we did. Ira Wingate III stood beside Niccolini. After the formalities, Scherer ordered Niccolini held without bail.

"No bail, Your Honor?" Wingate shouted. "Mr. Niccolini was almost three thousand miles away when this crime took place. Three time zones."

"There is ample reason for me to order no bail here, Mr. Wingate. This crime involves the brutal murder of two innocent people."

"My client has only been imprisoned once. And that was twelve years ago. He's a regular churchgoer. An ankle monitor and home detention would be more than sufficient."

"Request denied. Officers, take him away."

The court officers handcuffed Niccolini and led him off. As they walked him past us, Tony said to him, "Bye-bye, Angelo. I hear the food in the city jail is better than it used to be, but I'd stay away from pasta. They only use Ronzoni."

I then drove over to Roger Williams Park to meet Alex. He had been doing the usual: asking people who lived near there if they had seen or heard anything out of the ordinary. I joined him for another six houses. Nothing. It was almost twelve thirty, so I decided to knock off for lunch. Alex had to go to the Little War Shoppe, so I called Jimmy to see if he wanted to have lunch with me. He said he could meet me in an hour. We decided to meet at a Korean barbecue place that was near the Brown campus.

"The thing to have here is the dumplings," I said as we sat down.

"My doctor and Dolores is on my ass about eating too much meat."

"They have quite a few that don't have meat in them. Vegetable tofu…just look at the menu."

After we ordered, Jimmy began to tell me what angle he was working on. A few years before I joined the force, he had broken a big rape case. Three women had been assaulted. They had been pulled into an alley, chloroformed, and then viciously raped. They all worked in offices in the midtown area. The attacks took place when they were heading home after working late. Jimmy got the idea that there might be a connection between the women and the rapist. He checked everything from where they lived to where they ate lunch. Then he hit it. They all bought their shoes in the same store. A clerk in the store had followed them to their offices.

"So that's what I'm working on. Where the Angels ate, had their hair done, bought their booze. I haven't turned up anything yet, but I've just started. How are you guys coming?"

I told him we were at the same place. A few minutes later, our vegetable and pork dumplings were served in bamboo baskets, and we went through them like we had just been rescued from a lifeboat. Jimmy talked about Dolores, and it was easy to see that he hadn't been this happy in years. He wanted the four of us to get together for dinner. I told him as soon as Molly finished the play, we'd do it.

"I'm going to talk to you about something you don't want to hear."

"I know what it is. Is there any way I can derail you?"

"No. I've been speaking to Kitty about it for a couple weeks. Did you know that she's putting Perkins and Granger on Linda's murder?"

"When did she tell you that?"

"Yesterday."

"She's wrong."

"Danny, I haven't spoken to anyone who's been involved in this Angel business who thinks Linda was one of the victims. Just like those kids you nailed who tried to fake a murder by dressing up the victim to look like an angel. Someone else murdered Linda. I think it was someone who knew her."

Jimmy kept on about Linda. I tried to get him onto something else, but it didn't work. Then he said something that scared me. Big-time. He wanted me to work with him on it.

"There are enough people working on the Angels. If I'm wrong about Linda, then the others will reel him in. What do you say?" I spent a while trying to form words, but I wasn't able to say anything. Jimmy reached out and put his hand on my shoulder. "Okay. Let's table that. You have to do what feels right. I've always been an in-your-face kind of shmuck. Dolores says I start out in third gear."

Finally I was able to pull it together.

"You might be right, Jimmy, but I don't think I could work with you on it. At least not right away."

I don't know how, but thankfully we got on to talking about the Celtics and the Bruins and quickly finished lunch. I drove back to the park to meet Alex. When I got there, no Alex. I checked my cell, and there were two messages, both from Molly. I called her back and, surprise, surprise, I got her.

"It was great to see you last night. Any chance of doing it again tonight?"

"We have a tech tonight. God knows when it will end. You will be there on Friday for our opening, won't you?"

"Are you kidding me? Of course I will."

"There's a party afterward. I have to show up. At least for a short while—then I thought we could go to my place. I put a bottle of champagne in the fridge this morning. Good stuff. Roederer. Can't wait to see you."

CHAPTER FORTY-THREE

THURSDAY AND Friday Alex and I beat around the park and the street where Gayle Morse, the latest victim, had picked up her tricks. We developed a few leads that turned to shit. That was it.

"I just had a thought," I said to Alex as we got in the car.

"I'm all ears," he said as he adjusted the rearview mirror to comb his hair.

"Let's talk to LaVelle. Maybe the latest had a pimp."

"Sure. We should tell Kitty to pull all of them in."

"She rounded up a lot after the second one. Got nothing out of it."

"Well, at least LaVelle is fun."

We found LaVelle at a KFC on Wickenden.

"Well, looky, looky, looky. Today must be my lucky day. The two best-looking detectives on the PPF have come to call on me. I am truly fortunate." LaVelle led us to a table in the back. "How can I help you, gentlemen?"

"Take a guess," I said.

"Of course—the lovely white tree climber. I imagine a photo like that sells newspapers."

"Did you know her?" asked Alex.

"Never had the pleasure, Detective Larch."

"Did she have a pimp?" I asked.

"The name that's bouncing around is Big Shondell. You know him?"

"Three hundred pounds, platinum dreads, tat of Ray Charles on his neck?"

"That's your boy, Detective Martell."

"Where does he hang?"

"You know a bar called Bro and Bro?"

"Over on Pine?" asked Alex.

"No. That's the Broken Axe. This place is on Hope, near Doyle."

"Think he'd be there now?" I asked.

"The place is his office. If he's not sleeping or on the street, he's there."

Bro and Bro was sandwiched between a Laundromat and a shoe store. The shoe store had a large SPACE FOR RENT sign in its window, as did four other stores on the block. There was a neon sign above the door that said BR AND RO. We went in. The place was as dark as a movie house, though there was no problem picking out Big Shondell. We had run a check on him while diving over: given name, Tyrone Wilson; thirty-one; two arrests for dealing grass in the nineties, three for shoplifting, and one for car theft when he was a kid. Did a total of seven months for all of them.

"How are you, Shondell?" Alex asked.

"Only my friends call me that. You can call me Mr. Wilson."

"We'll have to remember that," I said. I took out a photo of the last Angel and showed it to him. "You know this girl?"

He squinted at it. "Yeah."

"When did you see her last?"

"Two, maybe three weeks ago."

"Did she work for you?" asked Alex.

"For a minute or two when she hit town. Too strung out to work much. Not worth it."

"Anyone else handle her?"

"Doubt it."

"Boyfriend?"

"You kidding? This kid was strung out. I mean, like, on a clothesline. The only friend she had was her dealer."

"Who was that?"

"Anyone she could find. I hope you guys are getting close to finding this mother. He's driving away business. Me and the boys are working on this, too. We know the street, and we're working it hard. It won't look too good for you if we find the creep first."

"Shondell—I mean, Mr. Wilson—I think you're right," I said as we got up and left.

That night at seven thirty was the opening of Molly's play, *The Changeling*. I had never seen it before. The program said it was written in 1622 by Middleton and Rowley, who I'd never heard of. In the audience I spotted three or four women from the outreach program. I had a little trouble following the dialogue, but I have that with Shakespeare, too.

Molly looked great, though her figure was hidden by a floor-length gown that you could have hidden half a kindergarten class under. Her voice was strong, but she didn't lose her natural warmth. She had the lead female role, and only the guy who played her father and the villain, De Flores, played by Brooks Shelby's brother, had bigger parts. The audience really responded, and the cast took three curtain calls.

"You were great," I told Molly as I hugged her in the dressing room she shared with four other women in the production.

"You're only saying that for the champagne I'm going to pour later."

While Molly took off her costume and removed her makeup, I walked down to the stage, where a table had been set up as a bar with bottles of wine and scotch and a line of paper cups.

"What can I get you?" asked Brooks Shelby, who was one of the three behind the bar.

"Red wine would be fine."

"I'd recommend the white," he said in a low voice. "It's from Chile, and it's a lot better than the red."

The white was dry and perfectly chilled. I quickly had a second. The stage rapidly filled up with cast, crew, and friends. I finally spotted Molly. She was with Miles Shelby.

"I think you've met Miles," she said and gave me a kiss on the cheek. I went from feeling good to feeling very good.

"That was a terrific performance," I said to him.

"Thanks. Your friend here wasn't bad either. Molly really has talent. We won't have her in Providence too much longer. She's going on to bigger things."

"Meaning?" I asked.

"Why, New York, of course. Or LA."

"That sounds great, but I still have things I'd like to do here."

"Such as?"

"I wouldn't mind playing the role of Hedda in the next production."

"Teddy Ashmead, an old friend of mine, is scheduled to direct. If you don't mind, I'd like to put in a word for you."

"Oh, Miles, you don't have to do that."

"I don't, but I want to."

A moment later, Miles was pulled away by a couple of people from the cast, and Molly and I started to make a slow circle of the party. For Molly there were kisses and more kisses. She went from beaming to radiant.

"I'd say this was a pretty good night for you."

Molly turned and faced me. She put her hands on my shoulders and gave me a long, deep kiss. This was not a secret kiss. I knew that at least half the people there were watching.

"It's even better than that. You know why?" She kissed me again. "Because you're here with me. What do you think I want to do now?" All I could do was just look at her. "I want to go to my place and turn the lights down, sit real close to you on the couch, and drink a lot of champagne. How does that sound to you?" I knew I'd have trouble answering, so I just kissed her.

Molly's apartment was small and minimally furnished, but the lights were dim, the champagne chilled, and her body pressed against mine felt just right. We stayed that way long enough to finish the champagne.

"I want to see if I can read your mind," she said.

"I'm starting to believe there's nothing you can't do."

"I think if I presented you with the choice of either my going to the fridge and getting another bottle of champagne or going with me into my bedroom, you'd pick the bedroom."

"You *are* a mind reader," I said. I kissed her and then stood up and carried her into the bedroom. We took off each other's clothes. We did it slowly, with only a minimum of fumbling. We were gentle with each other, and later, when I looked over at the clock in the bedside table, I couldn't believe that it was almost five in the morning.

"That was pretty good, Detective. Do you have to go home?"

"There's no chance of that."

"Then how about a few minutes of spooning?"

"If it leads to where I hope it does, let's take out the cloth and start polishing."

CHAPTER FORTY-FOUR

WHERE THE *fuck am I?* was my first thought. I had a mild, dull pain that ran from behind my left ear, right over my head—as if it had been drawn by a compass—to my other ear. Was it the champagne or the vodka I'd had at my place before going to the theater? The room was dark, but some light crept in from the bottom of the curtains. I reached across the bed. No Molly. I switched on the bedside light. I looked at the tabletop. No note. And then she walked in.

"Somebody needed a bit of recoup sleep. How do you feel?"

"If you take my head out of the equation, pretty good."

"You did hit the bubbles a bit last night. I seem to remember you did pretty well with the wine, too. Was the bed comfortable enough for you?"

"It was okay, but you were better."

"For that, you deserve a little morning surprise."

She handed me a small paper bag. NORATO was printed on the outside.

"How did you know?" I asked.

"That it's one of your favorite coffee places on Federal Hill? You've only mentioned it a dozen times."

"How'd you get there?"

"Took your car. I love it. You can park anywhere."

"You sound like my father."

"That's a little scary. I was trying to sound sultry, since I've realized that I don't have a class until eleven. Why don't you drink that coffee and then invite me back into bed. I thought we could take up where we left off."

Later, when I kissed Molly goodbye, I realized that I hadn't felt this good for a long, long time.

When I stopped for gas, I saw that there was a message on my cell from Alex. He wanted me to meet him at the Cask and Keg, a liquor store on Winslow. A clerk who worked there might have seen our guy.

"Is there something wrong?" he asked when I met him outside the store.

"Why?"

"You're smiling. I haven't seen that in a while."

I had no intention of telling him anything about Molly, so I told him I had just heard something funny on the radio. If I were really double-jointed, I would have kicked myself in the ass. Boy, was that lame. Luckily Alex didn't push me on it.

There were three men behind the counter.

"I'm Detective Larch. Is Ira Zellnick here?"

"That's me," said a short, overweight man in his forties with only a corona of hair, which was dyed crow black.

"Is there a place we can talk?"

"Right here is fine, Officer. Tino and Eddie both know what I told the patrolman."

"Well," I said, "why don't you tell us?"

"The night before that body was found in the tree, guy came in here and bought a bottle of vodka. Grey Goose. A quart. He looked like he spent a lot of time in the gym. The kind of guy who monopolizes the weight machines."

"What did he look like?" asked Alex.

"I had two other customers waiting, so I really didn't look at him closely. Forties, I think. Maybe fifty. I just remember he was a big guy."

"What else?" asked Alex.

"His car was parked right in front. There was a girl in it. Young. With blond hair. She had the light on in the car."

"What make?"

"All I can tell you is, it was big. Maybe an SUV."

"Color?"

"Sorry. It was dark, and the streetlight's across the street."

"How'd he pay?" I asked.

"Cash."

We tried some other lines:

Clothes?

He was wearing an overcoat. Probably black. Though it could have been brown.

Facial hair?

No. But then again, maybe he had a thin mustache.

Hair color?

Didn't notice.

Height?

Average.

That was enough. We thanked Mr. Zellnick and left.

"That was a big help," I said as we got in my car.

"That guy couldn't spot a bear in a lineup of penguins. Lunch?"

"Great idea. I heard about a new place on Olney. Thai. Supposed to be good."

"Sold."

We had just ordered when I heard my cell. It was Kitty.

"I'm at Saint Joseph's Hospital. In the ICU. Get over here as fast as you can."

"We'll be there in ten."

"Make it five."

CHAPTER FORTY-FIVE

KITTY WAS with Stuie Applebaum and Steve Rubino, who were both from the Third, in the waiting room outside the ICU. There was an older couple holding hands in the corner and two women crying softly on the other side of the room.

"I think we should talk in the hall," said Kitty.

"Can we do this outside?" asked Rubino. "I could use a cigarette."

"Okay, Steve, but you're not going to see your pension if you keep it up."

When we got outside, Kitty told Applebaum to lay it out for us.

"Guy's name is Wayne Tutlow. He was found in an alley next to the Walk Right Inn on Jessup. Badly beaten. Big-time. He's in a coma, but the doctors think there's a chance he'll pull out of it. Odds are fifty-fifty."

"The guy's got a rap sheet you could frame," said Rubino. "Served a total of almost nine in Mass and Delaware. Armed robbery and assault mainly. Beat two rape charges. In one the woman refused to testify at trial. Mass cops think she was paid off by Tutlow's family. The other one just disappeared."

"You think he's tied in to the Angels?" asked Alex.

"Yes," said Kitty.

"Why?" I asked.

Kitty reached into her pocket and took out an envelope. She handed it to me.

"Let's walk over here." I followed her to a bench near the parking lot. "Open it," she said.

It had some weight. I knew there was more than a note inside. I ripped it open and took out a woman's gold watch. I didn't have to turn it over to read the inscription on the back. I knew what it said: *From D. to L. With a love that keeps growing.* If I were alone, I would have started to cry. But I didn't. I was a cop, and I had a part I had to play.

"Is that Linda's?" Kitty asked.

"Yes," I heard myself say. "I gave it to her on our first anniversary. Where'd you get it?"

"It was in Tutlow's jacket pocket."

"Anything else?"

"Yes. Two of her credit cards, Visa and AmEx, and her bank card."

"How long has he been in town?"

"Don't know," she said. "Last time he had to report to a parole officer was two years ago. We just found out he was renting a room on Belnord."

"Has it been tossed yet?"

"No. That's what I want the four of you to do. Stuie has the address."

"How long was he there?"

"Just under two months."

"But the Angel business started before that."

"So what?" said Kitty. "He might have been staying somewhere else."

And then we heard, "Captain Berkowitz, Captain Catherine Berkowitz, please see Dr. Yulin in the ICU" on the hospital PA system. I followed Kitty back inside. The guys were right behind us. A tall, thin man with a thick red mustache was waiting for us outside the ICU. He was wearing a blue operating-room gown.

"Captain Berkowitz?" he asked Kitty.

"Yes, Doctor. This is Detective—"

"I don't have time for introductions, Captain. Mr. Tutlow is being prepped, and I have to operate immediately. He has a lot of bleeding, which causes pressure on the brain. We'll also be removing three hematomas."

"We were told that his chances are fifty-fifty."

"At best. It's a miracle that he's still alive."

"If he makes it, how long before we can talk to him?"

"I have no idea. What I can tell you is that you don't need to have one of your patrolmen guarding him outside his room. He's not going anywhere for a while."

The four of us headed over to Tutlow's place. Kitty went back to the station house. There were three rooming houses on the street, and Tutlow's was the crummiest. You could sense that the manager (his name tag said BIG SID), a short guy with a pencil behind each ear, liked to run his mouth, but he didn't have much to tell us.

"When did he take the place?" Rubino asked.

"The seventeenth. That's a little over two months ago."

"Did he tell you where he stayed before?"

"No. He was a real closemouthed guy. I couldn't even get him to talk about the Sox."

"Did you ever see him with anybody else?"

"No. He was a loner. I didn't see him with anybody."

As we walked up to room 407, Alex whispered to me, "Maybe the boys should go in first. You know, check things out."

I didn't even answer. I just kept walking up the stairs.

"Jesus," said Rubino as we walked in, "somebody open a window. This place stinks."

The room, unfortunately, had its own bathroom, and that, combined with the smell of Chinese takeout food—there were empty containers all over the place—and cheap cologne, created a real miasma. Applebaum, holding a handkerchief to his nose, went into the bathroom and flushed the toilet by pushing down on the lever with his shoe. He then closed the door. Alex opened both windows.

It didn't take long to go through the room. There was one small closet and an old, battered dresser. We found a thirty-eight short wrapped in a T-shirt in the bottom drawer. That was about it until Alex looked under the bed. There he found a small suitcase. He pulled it out and opened it. On top were some dirty shirts and socks. He turned it over and dumped the contents on the bed.

"Well, look what we have here," said Applebaum.

We were looking at women's underwear. Rubino opened an evidence bag and, using a pencil, started to pick up a bra.

"Stop," I said. "Let me see that."

The bra was pale blue. It looked almost new, because it was. I had been with Linda when she bought it. How did I know it was hers? She always put a number with a black felt pen on the strap so she could keep track of how often she wore it. It couldn't have been washed more than once or twice, because the number 7 was still dark.

"What's up, Danny?" asked Alex.

"Nothing. I thought maybe we could pick up a print on the clasp. But it's too small."

"The lab will check them for DNA," said Rubino.

Why didn't I tell them that I knew it was Linda's? I don't know. Maybe I thought we had enough already. Maybe I didn't want to share that with Applebaum and Rubino, or even Alex. The only person I knew that I'd talk to about it was Jimmy Warden. No one else.

CHAPTER FORTY-SIX

I GOT home that night around seven. I didn't shop because I knew there was enough in the fridge for dinner. But I didn't want to cook, and I didn't want to eat alone. I called Molly first.

"Oh, Danny, I wish you'd called me an hour ago. I'm having dinner with Ginger after the show."

"You can't get out of it?"

"I really can't. She covered for me when I was rehearsing the play."

Then I called Jimmy.

"Sure. I'm grabbing a bite with Dolores and then catching the new Coen brothers movie. Why don't you come along?"

"I don't feel like a movie. Actually I just wanted to talk to you."

"About what?"

"Tutlow."

"Who?"

"That's right—you don't know. Why don't we get together tomorrow and I'll fill you in."

"Great. By the way, could you give me a list of the people in that outreach program at the church?"

"Sure."

"How many are there?"

"About a dozen."

"And how many are guys?"

"Three or four. I really only know one of them. Why?"

"I have an idea. It probably won't pan out, but…"

"But what?"

"I have to go. That's Dolores at the door. We'll talk tomorrow."

I poured myself a vodka and turned on the tube. I surfed a dozen channels before settling on a replay of *Charlie Rose* from the night before. He was talking to a guy with dyed black hair that was greased and combed up to resemble a wave about to crest. It took another minute for me to figure out that he was a designer and another for me to turn it off. Then the phone rang.

"What are you doing?"

It was Alex.

"Not much."

"How about going out for a bite with me?"

"I thought this was a war-game night."

"It is, but two of the guys couldn't make it. Bad colds."

"Where do you want to go?"

We settled on a new Chinese place near the river. We were on our second drink when Alex told me that he was seeing someone.

"Serious?"

"Sort of."

"Anyone I know?"

"You've met her once."

"I'm not good at guessing games. Who the fuck is it?"

"Remember the gal from JetBlue?"

"Karen."

"You have a good memory."

"It's not hard remembering someone that attractive."

As the meal progressed—the food was pretty good—we talked about the Sox, our IRAs, and new cars (his lease was running out in a few months), until we finally got to Tutlow.

"I think we found our guy. Kitty thinks so, too."

"It sort of looks that way."

"What was going on with you and Kitty this morning at the hospital?"

"She wanted to tell me about Linda's stuff that they found on Tutlow. She didn't want to do it in front of you guys."

"It would be great to wrap this up," he said. I motioned to the waitress for another drink. "I think it will help to put this behind you."

What the fuck was he talking about? How do you put the murder of your wife behind you? Sometimes Alex could sound like someone who majored in Dr. Phil. Luckily my drink came quickly, and I was able to shift the conversation over to Alex's new workout routine. Lately that was his favorite topic.

CHAPTER FORTY-SEVEN

WHEN I came into the precinct house Monday morning, I stopped at Kitty's office.

"Is everything okay, Captain?" I asked.

Her eyes were clown red and beyond puffy. She kept dabbing at them with a balled-up Kleenex. She started to talk and then stopped. A moment later came the tears, big ones, the kind that produces hiccups. I went around the desk and started to pat her on the back. When she finally caught her breath, she said, "Cuffs." Cuffs? What the hell did she mean? "He was such a beauty."

Of course! It was her cat Cuffs.

"What happened?"

"I had to put him down…this morning."

"I'm sorry. That's terrible," I said as I continued to pat her on the back.

It took a while, but she finally pulled herself together a bit. Then she gave me the whole story and then some: the weight loss, the listlessness, the hair falling out. Yesterday after work she had taken him in to the vet, and the diagnosis was beyond grim. Riddled with cancer. I've never been much of a cat person—my brother and I had three dogs growing up; one was hit by a car, one ran away, and the other died when I was in college—but I felt for Kitty.

"Could you do me a favor, Danny?"

"Anything. What do you need?"

"Cuff's ashes are at Maxfield's on Montrose. Could you pick them up for me? I don't think I'm up to it."

"Sure. Is there anything else I can do?"

She nodded and then stood up and hugged me. Luckily, when she sat back down, Alex walked in.

"Hey, guys."

"The Captain's busy," I said as I headed to the door.

"Jesus, Kitty didn't look good," he said as we walked down the hallway.

"Yeah. I think someone in her family isn't well."

"Where do you want to head?"

"I think she'd like us to check on Tutlow at the hospital. Applebaum and Rubino were there yesterday. No change."

"Let's go."

When we got there, we couldn't find the doctor who had operated on Tutlow, but a nurse pointed out the resident who was in charge of the floor.

"Tutlow? Let me get his chart," said the doctor, whose name tag read MEHTA.

We walked with him to the nurses' station. He scanned the chart.

"He's beginning to come out of it. Dr. Segal removed two hematomas. There were two additional ones. Because of the location of the subarachnoid hemorrhages, he opted to leave them alone. They're starting to dissolve."

"When do you think we might be able to talk to him?"

"I can't answer that. Maybe in a day or two, a week, or maybe never."

"Never?"

"Yes, Detective Martell. He might come out of the coma without the ability to speak. This man suffered severe trauma."

As we walked to the car, Alex's cell phone rang. It was Johnnie Gallagher, who manned the desk at the precinct house.

"Yeah, Johnnie. What's up?...Where? When did it happen?... We're on our way."

Alex started to trot. "Shooting," he said over his shoulder. "Doubleheader. Just found them in a garage. Over on Arlington and Lloyd. We're the closest."

When we got there, only two squad cars were out in front of the six-story redbrick building. A good-looking young female officer was standing on the steps outside.

"Hi. Follow me."

"What's your name, Officer?" asked Alex. "Haven't seen you around."

"Niven. Cindy Niven. I just joined the force six weeks ago."

"Have you handled a shooting before?" he asked.

We followed her into the hallway and then down a flight of stairs to the garage. Alex was right behind her, staring at her ass like a school crossing guard watching a group of second-graders cross a busy street.

"No, sir."

"Who called it in?" I asked.

"The janitor. He's waiting downstairs."

As we pushed open the door to the garage, I could hear the sirens of a few more cars and the wail of an ambulance arriving.

"Oh, shit," said Alex as he got to the car, a black SUV. I stood next to him, and for a moment, I couldn't say anything. It was the Flea, his forehead resting against the steering wheel like he was napping, a large Rorschach bloodstain on the collar of his shirt. Next to him was his girlfriend, Yolanda. She had been shot in the temple. Blood was sprayed on the windshield and all over the front-seat cushion. There were no bullet holes in the car's windows. The killer must have been inside the car with them.

"At least his cornrows weren't fucked up," said Alex.

"When was he supposed to testify in the Sands case?"

"In two weeks."

"I think our first stop is a visit to our favorite slumlord."

"I'll bet Bernie's out of town. Just like Nardini."

"Yeah. Probably been away for at least a week," I said.

We stayed there for almost an hour, until three detectives from our precinct and the coroner arrived. Of course when we got to Bernie Sands's office, he wasn't there. His secretary, a good-looking redhead (Alex got her phone number before we left), told us that Bernie was in Florida, visiting his sick mother.

"When did he leave, Tami?" asked Alex.

"Last Wednesday."

"And when will he be back?"

"Day after tomorrow."

I handed her my card. "Tell him to give me a call as soon as he gets in. I mean I want him to make it his first call. Tell him it's very important. Got it?"

When we got back, I told Alex I had to see Kitty. Alex said that he'd start on our report. Kitty was in with Lawson, so I had to wait at least twenty minutes.

"I heard you went to see Sands," she said.

"Yeah. And he wasn't there."

"Big surprise."

"Supposedly he gets back tomorrow. We'll be on him as soon as he gets off the plane."

"You haven't picked up Cuffs yet, have you?"

"No. I'm going to do it after I get off. When I'm alone."

"Thanks, Danny. You know he was just two months shy of seventeen."

"That sounds pretty old."

"I had one that hit twenty-one. But Cuffs was a very special little guy."

"Now, I have a favor to ask of you, Captain."

"Name it."

"When we set up Sands, one of the tenants who was being harassed really helped us out. Her name's Molly Juste. She's become a friend of mine. A good friend."

I went on to tell her that Molly was scheduled to testify in the Sands case, and now, after the Flea's killing, I was worried about her.

"What do you want me to do? Put a car in front of her building at night?"

"Yes."

"Danny, I can't do that. We don't have the manpower. What I can do is have a car take a pass at her building twice every hour from sunset till sunup. That's the best I can do."

"That would be great, Captain."

"I've heard from Jimmy Warden that this Molly is a very nice lady. You've been through a lot, and I'm glad you've found a good woman to spend some time with. You don't have to tell her about the Flea, but it would be a good idea to have her stay with you for a while."

A couple of hours later when I left, Alex asked me in the parking lot if I wanted to have a drink. I told him I had to meet someone for dinner. I was smiling when I pulled out of the lot. It would have been fun instead to say that I had a date with Cuffs.

CHAPTER FORTY-EIGHT

THAT NIGHT, Molly came to my place for dinner. We decided to share the cooking. The night was mild, so I decided to grill. I'd do pork chops and the side, scalloped potatoes. Molly would handle the salad and dessert. I was hoping she'd agree to a sleepover. It wasn't warm enough to eat outside, so we compromised by setting the table in the sun porch, which still had the storm windows in place. The porch looked out on the garden in the back. A few years before, Linda had hired an outdoor-lighting guy to light the trees and shrubs. I thought the expense was ridiculous. But I was wrong. The place looked magical at night. Molly brought over a bottle of wine, a Shiraz from Chile, which went perfectly with the meal. Molly and I had reached the point where we didn't have to talk all the time. So when we did, we bounced around easily: from a scene (*The Glass Menagerie*) she was preparing for a class to a novel by Evelyn Waugh that she had given me the week before. I was a hundred pages into it and was liking it a lot. I had never heard of him. In fact, I had thought Evelyn was a woman until I saw the author's photo on the back cover. I stayed away from talking about Tutlow, and, luckily, I didn't have to answer any questions about the Flea. The paper had run a medium-size piece on the murders but hadn't included a picture of him. Molly didn't know his name, and since there was also no mention of the Bernie Sands trial, the whole thing didn't register with her.

"What are you thinking about?" she asked as I poured more wine into her glass.

"You."

"That takes in either a lot or a little."

"I'd put my chips on a lot." I got up and went around the table. I leaned down and kissed her neck. "Any chance I can get you to stay here tonight?"

She pulled me down and kissed me deeply.

"How's that for an answer?"

"I have an idea. Let's leave everything and clean up tomorrow."

We hardly said another word until we finally went to sleep a few hours later. Around five I woke up to take a leak. Molly was deeply asleep. She was a two-pillow sleeper—one for her head and one to hug—and almost seemed to be smiling. The bathroom was next to a room that I used as an office. I went in to see if I had any e-mail. There was the usual dog pack of spam: watches for sale, insurance for almost everything, and hard-on pills from Canada. But there was also one from Kitty. She had sent it about the time we had sat down for dinner:

"Danny: Tutlow has regained consciousness. He can talk! The surgeon will meet us at 8:30. I want you to be there with me. No Alex. No one else. No need to e-mail me back. Just be there. K."

I got to the hospital at exactly eight thirty, and Kitty wasn't there. She showed up five minutes later. She handed me a coffee. The side of the cup said NORATO'S.

"I know you like good coffee. This is a very small repayment for what you did for Cuffs."

A moment later Dr. Yulin walked over.

"Good morning, Captain," he said.

"We're going to see Tutlow."

"Mr. Tutlow is a very lucky man. Most people don't survive that kind of beating. His skull was broken in two places. He was probably beaten with a baseball bat."

"You said he could talk, didn't you?"

"Yes. He's still a bit slow, but he can understand and express himself well enough for you to question him. My only proviso is that you keep it short. He's very tired."

Tutlow's room was at the end of the hall. A uniformed officer from the Second was seated in a chair by the door.

"Rob," said Kitty as we opened the door, "no one comes in until we're finished."

Arlene Cornick, our video technician, was adjusting the lights when we walked into the room. Tutlow, his head covered by what looked like a white plaster helmet, was sipping some water through a glass hospital straw. His face was drawn and almost as pale as the sheet that came up to his shoulders.

"I hope Dr. Yulin told you that this shouldn't take too much time. Mr. Tutlow really needs rest," said a short, heavy nurse who was adjusting Tutlow's IV.

"We won't take long. And I'd appreciate it if you'd leave the room when we interview Mr. Tutlow." The nurse gave her a nasty look and left. "Are you ready, Arlene?" Kitty asked the video technician.

"All set, Captain."

Kitty and I stood at the foot of the bed.

"Mr. Tutlow, my name is Captain Catherine Berkowitz, and this is Detective Daniel Martell. We want to talk to you about some items we found on your person and also at your apartment."

Tutlow's voice was thin, and he had only two responses to Kitty's questions: "I don't know what the fuck you're talking about" and "I have no fucking idea."

After ten minutes Tutlow nodded off. Kitty told Arlene to pack up her equipment. As we walked to our cars, Kitty asked me if I wanted to have breakfast.

"What do you have in mind?" I asked.

"There's a new place I've heard good things about that's only a few blocks from here. It's called The Morning Garden. Good, fresh food, and yes, they also serve bacon and eggs. Though their coffee is decidedly American. What do you say?"

The place looked good: baskets of fresh fruits and vegetables lined a table by the front door, and a huge, glass-fronted fridge, crammed with bottles of milk and cream, was set against the opposite wall.

We both ordered OJ. It was fresh squeezed and chilled just right. When I put my empty glass down, Kitty leaned over, put her hand on mine, and looked me in the eye.

"Tutlow didn't do it."

"What did you say?"

"Tutlow didn't kill Linda."

"Is this a joke?"

"No. I haven't told anyone. I've had three guys on it since we found him in the alley. He couldn't have killed her. He was in a cell on Rikers Island on a gun charge. He did four months there and didn't get out until three weeks after Linda was murdered."

"Then how did Linda's watch and credit cards get into his pocket? And what about her stuff that we found in his room?"

"When we find that out, we'll find out who really killed Linda."

"None of this makes any sense. Why would someone want to frame Tutlow?"

"I don't know."

"Both Alex and Jimmy thought from the beginning that Linda was not part of the Angel business. And now I'm starting to think they may have been right."

CHAPTER FORTY-NINE

LATER THAT afternoon Alex and I went to the conference room, where our new big-screen TV was set up. The Flea team was waiting for us: Kirby and Fontana from the Third, and Robbins and Deal from our precinct. We were there to look at the DVD from one of the security cameras that had been set up in the Flea's garage. One of the tech guys had scanned it and cut out everything that had been recorded before the Flea drove into the garage. Robbins put the DVD in the player, and I turned off the lights. We watched the Flea's car pull into his spot. Nothing happened for at least a minute.

"Did you see that?" asked Fontana.

"See what?" answered Alex.

"I think it was a flash. Inside the car."

"Hey, Robby," I said. "Go back to the beginning, please."

Fontana was right. There was a flash. Actually, two. Then the back door opened and a man got out. We couldn't make out his face, but he was wearing a white cowboy hat. We looked at it a couple more times but couldn't find anything else.

"It's what we thought," I said to Alex. "No holes in the windows."

"Let's divvy this up," said Deal. "Robbins and I have an arraignment downtown in a half hour."

Since Alex and I had dealt with him, we took Bernie Sands. Kirby and Fontana took the Flea's building and the surrounding neighborhood, and Robbins and Deal the restaurant where the

Flea had dinner (they had found an AmEx receipt in his jacket pocket). The key, of course, was the guy in the cowboy hat.

Bernie Sands's office was near the Brown campus. The Sands Property Group was located in the basement of one of his few upscale buildings. The reception area had just a couple of tabletop desks and four straight-backed chairs. Behind both desks were guys. Big guys. It was easy to spot that these boys weren't traditional secretaries when one of the gorillas greeted us with, "What do you guys want?"

"Bernie Sands," Alex said as we both flashed our badges.

"He's busy," said Gorilla #2.

"Maybe you have a slight hearing problem. We want to see him now. If that can't be arranged, I think we might have to check you two out. Our computer records are pretty up-to-date. Maybe you have an outstanding jaywalking ticket? Perhaps something a little more serious?"

That was enough. Gorilla #2, who probably had more than a misdemeanor outstanding, got up and motioned us to follow him down the hall.

Bernie Sands was seated behind a large beat-up desk that was covered with papers and files. He gave us a big smile as we walked in.

"Good to see you, guys. I guess you're here to celebrate with me."

"What the fuck you talking about, slimeball?" said Alex.

"The Flea. I want to buy him a gift. A big one. If you tell where they're planting the fat fuck, I'll get something nice and leave it on his grave."

"You're very funny, Bernie," I said. "I bet you'll have even better material when you're indicted on Murder One."

"That's not going to happen. The Flea had a lot of enemies. I might have wished him dead, but I had nothing to do with it. And maybe you haven't heard about my indictment. It was dropped this morning. So, all in all, it's been a very good morning."

We went at him for a half hour and could get nothing out of him. He wasn't a dumb guy, and we both knew that there was only one way we could get to Sands: we needed to find the man in the white cowboy hat.

CHAPTER FIFTY

THE NEXT morning the six of us met in Kitty's office to fill her in. So far none of us had turned up anything. Yes, the Flea had been at the restaurant with his girlfriend and a man in a white cowboy hat. The maître d', waiter, and coat-check girl all agreed on that. The problem was that their descriptions of the cowboy all differed wildly. The waiter thought he was Asian, while the maître d' thought he was a dead ringer for Sonny Bono. That was as close to an agreement as they could get.

"Guys," said Kitty when we finished, "as you know, the charges against Bernie Sands have been dropped. The Flea was the absolute key to the case. The video and audio that we got in the diner turned out to be lousy. We bounced the video tech. Danny, the DA was thinking of having your friend Molly testify. But her contact was only with the Flea. So we dropped that. Now we have to nail Sands on this. Does anybody doubt that he was behind the Flea's murder?" No hands were raised. "Now, does anyone believe that one of our local wack artists would wear a cowboy hat on a job?" Our hands stayed in our laps. "So it's got to be someone from out of town. Way out of town. Aside from the usual phone and e-mail checks, does anybody have any ideas on where we go on this?"

"Sands obviously paid the guy in cash," said Fontana. "Let's check his accounts."

"Good idea, but that's for the trial. It won't help us find Mr. Hat. So what if he withdrew twenty-five grand or whatever? He'll say it was for some off-the-books work on one of his dives."

"I think I should hit some spots on Federal Hill with Tony LaMarco," I said. "Maybe he used local talent to contact someone outside to do the work. We had that with Nardini."

"It's worth a try," said Kitty. "Any other ideas?"

"We should check hotels and motels. Here and at the airport," said Alex. "We don't know what he looks like, but the white cowboy hat is certainly something that a desk clerk would remember."

"Good thinking. Now, let's meet back here at six. Please get me something, guys. If you don't, you'll get a good sampling of my coprolalia. Kirby and Fontana, definition, please." Since neither of them had ever been exposed to Kitty's word of the day, they just stared blankly at her. "What about the rest of you?"

"Don't have a clue, Captain," said Deal.

"I'm disappointed, gentlemen. *Coprolalia* means 'excessive or uncontrollable swearing.' So if you don't want to hear me curse, dig something up. We have to nail Sands."

Around three I got a call on my cell from Molly.

"Are you free for a movie tonight?"

"Depends on the time."

"There's a nine-ten show."

"Sure. What's the flick?"

"It's a French film. It won an award at Cannes."

"Where's it playing?"

"The Film Franchise on Benefit."

"See you there at eight thirty. We can have a drink first."

I got there at 8:20. No Molly. I had a copy of the *Boston Globe* with me, but I got through that in twenty minutes. Still no Molly. I tried calling her. Got her machine. I left a message: "Hey, there. You've got a cop who has been waiting for you for almost half an hour. Movie's set to start in ten minutes. Move it, please." Fifteen minutes later, I walked across the street and bought a copy of

Newsweek. I was into the book section when she arrived, smiling like she'd won the lottery.

"Will you forgive me?" she said after kissing me deeply.

"Kiss me again like that, and I'll forgive you for the next time, too."

"I have spectacular news, but I need a drink first."

"There's a pretty good burger place a few blocks down that has a bar."

"What are you waiting for? Let's go," she said as she grabbed my hand and pulled me down the street. When we got there, Molly did something I had never seen her do before: she ordered a martini. Gin, with only, as she told the bartender, "a suggestion of vermouth."

"That's a real drink," I said.

"Occasions like this deserve a real drink. I've got great news."

"I'm listening."

"I now have an agent. A real, well-known, important, film— and TV—agent."

"That's fantastic. You never mentioned anything to me."

"It just happened. He called me from LA. About an hour ago. His name is Barry Friedlich. He's the cochairman of International Artists Agency. I Googled him. He's the real thing. You won't believe his client list."

"How did he find out about you?"

"He was at the play. His daughter goes to Brown. She did the lighting."

Molly was more than bubbling over. She looked radiant. She told me that Friedlich had asked his daughter for a DVD of the play. He absolutely loved her performance. He thought he had a role for her on an NBC show called *Attack Squad*, which his agency had packaged—later she told me what that meant. He then gave the showrunner—she explained what that meant, too—the

DVD, and he also really liked Molly's performance. They planned to fly her out to LA in the next week or so for a test.

"That's fantastic," I said, which gave me the opportunity to kiss her again.

"This calls for more than burgers. We have to celebrate tonight. Let's go to Al Forno's. And I'm paying."

Before we sat down, Molly worked the room and told her friends about what had happened. This led to martinis magically appearing, followed by at least five courses. Ginny and Abe, who usually worked the same shift as Molly, brought over a bottle of Prosecco.

When we got in the car, I pulled her close and said, "I'm really happy for you. Really and truly. But promise me you won't move to Los Angeles."

"Don't worry about that, Danny Boy. Don't ever forget that you're a key part of both my career and my life."

I drove home very slowly and very carefully. I knew I didn't have to ask Molly if she was going to spend the night with me.

CHAPTER FIFTY-ONE

TONY AND I spent two days drinking espresso and talking to the "boys" on Federal Hill. The only thing we turned up was a tip on a new Sicilian restaurant in Narragansett and that a lot of them were really pissed about what happened to the Flea. All of them believed that Bernie Sands was involved. We heard quite a few times, "Someone should take care of Sands." Having the gorillas around was definitely a smart move on Sands's part. Just before five I got a call that Kitty wanted to see us. We headed in and found the rest of the team in her office.

"You can all knock off the Sands business," Kitty said when she walked into the office.

"What gives, Captain?" asked Alex.

"I got a call from a friend on the Boston PD. Bernie and one of his muscle boys bought it a few hours ago. In the parking lot at Fenway. A bomb attached to the starter of his car. It's probably on the tube right now. It's Boston's problem. I'm sure a call was placed from Federal Hill to a buddy in the North End and that was that. Three good things happened today: the Flea and his lady friend's murder was solved; Sands is not going to beat it; and now the Boston cops have to do the work. If I knew who did it, I'd thank them."

So would I, I thought. Now Molly was safe.

A couple of hours later, Jimmy Warden called me.

"How long you going to be at your desk?"

"At least another hour."

"Wait for me. I'm coming in."

Twenty minutes later Jimmy sat down opposite me.

"You look good. Still seeing the actress?"

"Yes. And you look good, too. What's on your mind, Jimmy?"

"Remember a little while back I asked you for a list of all the people in the church outreach group? Well, I need it now."

"Sure. I have a partial list here. I'm sorry it slipped my mind before—I'll give it to you now. It'll only take me a few days to get you a complete one. Why do you want it?"

"It's about those killings in Salisbury. I'm going back there tomorrow to kick the tires. How'd you like to drive there again with me?"

"That won't work. I'm tied up."

"Too bad."

"Say, did you hear about Bernie Sands catching it in Boston?"

"Yeah. It's all over the tube. They'll never nail the guy who did it, but I'll bet a fin it was Richie Malfi. He was always the guy who handled that stuff for the boys. He's a real artist with dynamite. Worked mainly for the Renzi brothers."

"Kitty had the same idea this morning. It didn't play out. Malfi is doing four to six in Walpole. But, as Kitty said, now it's Boston's problem."

I met my father that night for dinner at an Indian restaurant downtown. I had put it off twice, but I couldn't duck it after my mother called me to say how disappointed he had been when I backed out the last time. He greeted me with the now-obligatory hug.

"You look good, Danny."

"So do you, Dad. Did you work out today?"

"I only skip Sundays. I wish I had been like you when I was young. Might have missed all that heart business I went through."

We started talking about the usual stuff: the Sox, the election for mayor, which was starting to heat up. Thankfully he didn't bring up Linda.

"You were involved in that Bernie Sands case, weren't you?"

"Yeah, with Alex."

We then did a few minutes on Alex (my dad liked him) before we ordered drinks. Dad was a dedicated Johnnie Walker Red guy, while I ordered a chilled Absolut with three olives. We then endured a long pause, with me scrambling to a workable subject, but he beat me to it.

"When are we going to meet your friend Molly?"

"She's been busy."

"We know. We went to that play that she was in."

"You did?" I said with more than a hint of surprise.

"She's very attractive and very good."

I then surprised myself by quickly agreeing to take Molly to our next family Sunday lunch.

"I think you and Mom will like her."

"Well, your uncle and grandmother already do."

Then I was telling him about her getting an agent and going to LA for a test. That opened the floodgates. He wanted to know about the agent, the show, how to prepare for a screen test, and a score of other things that I couldn't answer. When he got off of showbiz, he switched to Molly's family: where they lived, when they got here (old-timers—early 1800s), where she went to school. He took a break to order another drink and then wanted to know if she was a reader, could she cook...By the time we said goodbye, I realized I had had a pretty good time. There had been, much to my surprise, no Linda talk. I agreed to go to a game with him and my brother the following week. Our hug as we turned to go to our cars felt good. Felt real.

"Hey, son," he called out when he was thirty feet away. "I forgot something."

"What was that, Dad?"

"That I'd really like it if you gave some thought to joining your brother and me someday. You're a terrific cop, but you're also a terrific lawyer."

CHAPTER FIFTY-TWO

"HE JUST called."

Molly's voice was just below a scream.

"Who called?"

"Barry. My agent. They want me to go to LA tomorrow."

Sunday morning at seven, I drove Molly to the airport. She first had to fly to New York to catch her flight to LA. She was still on a high from the day before.

"Did I tell you they're flying me business class?"

"Yes. And that you're staying at the Chateau Marmont. And, yes, I remember that's where John Belushi died."

"I'm starting to feel nervous, Danny."

"You're supposed to. You're going to be fine. In fact, you'll be terrific."

"You really think so?"

"You know I do."

I parked at the terminal, flipped down the sun visor with my PD ID, and walked her to security.

"I'd walk you to the gate, but I'm carrying a gun."

"Danny, I haven't said this enough. I love you."

We kissed for a long time. Long enough for one of the security guys to cough for us to get the idea that we were holding up the line.

As I drove back to my place—I didn't have to get in to the station until nine thirty—my cell phone rang. It was Alex.

"Larson just called me. They found another one. Grand Street. By the river. Kitty won't be there. She's out of town. Now her sister has an infection. I'll meet you down there."

CHAPTER FIFTY-THREE

HE COULD smell the river. It would be light in an hour. This Angel was really light. Grand Street came to a dead end at the river. There was a strip of small trees and brush between the street and the river. He walked in, and just as he was about to place the Angel on the ground and attach the wings, he stepped on something soft.

"What the hell are you doing?" a man shouted.

All he could do was drop the body and run to his car.

CHAPTER FIFTY-FOUR

THERE WERE eleven of us there when I arrived. The couple who found the body were off to the side, being questioned by Al and Jackie from the Third. Alex told me that the couple said they had been "stargazing" ("That's spelled *shtupping*," he said) when the Angel Killer almost walked over them.

"He just dropped the body. It was wrapped in a blanket. Wings were inside the blanket. Not attached yet. Finally we got something. It wasn't full light yet, but they saw him. White and big. A real muscle boy. They also saw his car: a Caddy. Black and pretty new. Since the guy owns a muffler shop, I think we can trust him."

When Larson finished with the ME, we grouped around him.

"Guys, this is really bad. We've asked the two witnesses to keep it buttoned, but I'm sure they won't. No one can resist having his face on the tube. So this is going to be even bigger than the tree job. This is four, right?"

"Five," said Tommy LaMarco.

"Jesus. I don't know where my head is this morning. The important thing is, we got the makings of a Green River serial killer here. The Boston press has been whacking off over this. I don't want it to jump to LA."

"Alex told me about the guy and the car. Do we have anything else?" I asked.

"Not much. This victim was white. Twenties, early thirties. Like the others, strangled. Made up the same way, too. We don't have an ID on her yet. She was probably murdered yesterday."

"Anything on the plate?"

"No. Too dark. But the guy thinks it was Connecticut."

"Connecticut?" said Alex.

"Don't bet the farm on that," said Larson.

"When is the Captain coming back?" I asked.

"Don't know. Her aunt, who raised her, is in the ICU. She's not going to make it. Kitty doesn't know when she'll pass."

We broke up and did our usual stuff: ringing bells and asking people if they had seen something when they were asleep. We all got back around four, and after an hour at our desks, cleaning up things, we met in Larson's office.

"We've identified the victim. Her name is Tanya Bohlen. Thirty-four. She owned a florist shop at two-two—"

"We know her!" Alex shouted out. "She was a volunteer at the outreach center at Father Coles's church."

"Yeah, we interviewed her at the beginning of this shit," I added. "A real nice lady."

"Well, she doesn't fit the profile at all," said Larson. "Danny, you and Alex go over to her place tomorrow morning. She lived above her store."

I had just poured a vodka when Molly called.

"I just had lunch downstairs. I ate outside. You know who was at the table next to mine?"

She sounded like a kid who had just sat on Santa's lap.

"Clark Gable."

"No. George Clooney. Really."

"Did he hit on you?"

"Of course not."

"Well, if he does, tell him you have a male friend who's armed."

"I wish you were here, Danny. I miss you a lot."

"Same here, baby."

She then named five more famous people she'd seen at the hotel—I'd heard of only one. She made me promise that I'd call her before I went to bed, and after a lot of "love yous," I finally said goodbye.

CHAPTER FIFTY-FIVE

I TRIED calling Jimmy on his cell to tell him about the latest Angel. Jimmy was very much into the outreach group and had to know as soon as possible about Tanya Bohlen.

Larson had arranged for her sister, Terry Bohlen Hodge, to meet us at her place. A tall, attractive woman with straight blond hair that was almost white opened the door. Her eyes, not surprisingly, were a raw red.

"Ms. Hodge, I'm Detect—"

"I know. Come on in."

"There's not much you can say at times like this," I said, "but we met your sister once at the church, and she was truly lovely. We're going to do all we can to catch the guy."

"I know you will, but that won't bring her back."

And then she started to cry. First just small, muffled sobs. Then a wail as she rocked back and forth. I handed her a handkerchief, and then we led her to a small couch in the living room. She cried so hard, she started to hiccup. Alex patted her on the back until she stopped.

"I'm sorry, it's just…"

"We understand," said Alex. "Did you speak to your sister before it happened?"

"The day before yesterday."

"Did she mention anything about the outreach center?"

"Yes. Something happened there that upset her. It was about a young woman who came in and suddenly ran out. She said she'd tell me about it the next day at lunch. But that never happened."

She started to cry again. This time it took her only a minute to pull herself together.

"We need to look through the apartment," I said. "Do you mind if we do it now?"

"No. But I think I'll go down to the shop. Jean, Tanya's assistant, might need some help."

The apartment had three rooms in addition to the kitchen: living room, bedroom, and study. I took the study. Since we knew that the chances were that Tanya wasn't attacked there, I didn't toss the room. I went through her desk carefully. I was looking for a journal or diary, or even any slip of paper that was tied to the woman who ran out of the center. Nothing. We met in the living room and went through that quickly. We didn't turn up a thing.

"We have to get all the outreach people together," I said.

"You're right. Let's go back and start calling."

It took us most of the morning to contact all the volunteers. There were fifteen of them, and we set the meeting for the next evening at seven. I was about to leave to meet Alex for lunch when Molly called.

"It's set. Tomorrow at eleven. It's on the Warner lot. I've never been to a studio before."

"You're going to be great. Have you memorized your lines?"

"Of course. It's only two and a half pages."

"Don't forget to call me when you finish."

"Are you kidding? You come before my mother. And whatever you do, don't wish me good luck."

"But I can send you love. And that's what I'm doing."

When I got home that night, there was a message from Kitty on the machine: "Danny, everything here is finished. Not easy, but I got through it better than I would have expected. I'll be in tomorrow. Larson filled me in on the new one. I have a feeling that we're going to nail him now. Alex told me about your meeting tomorrow with the outreach volunteers. I think I'd like to come along. We'll talk in the morning. Be good."

CHAPTER FIFTY-SIX

WE DIDN'T get to the outreach center until almost seven thirty Tuesday evening. As we were about to leave, a call came in from LaVelle. She said she might have something for us on the new Angel. We drove over to Mr. Bobby's, a bar on the block where LaVelle worked. It was the kind of place that if you were smart you wouldn't go near, but if you had to go, carrying a bat and a spear wouldn't be a bad idea. Cops are easy to spot, so the place got a lot quieter when we walked in.

"We're looking for LaVelle," Alex told the bartender.

"She just called up. She said she's busy with an important customer. She'll be here around eight. Drinks are on her," said the bartender.

"We can't wait around. Tell her to meet us tomorrow morning. She knows where to find us."

The outreach people were in a large meeting room off the basement dining area where the church served up meals for the homeless. Kitty was seated in the back. She was wearing a black ribbon on the lapel of her jacket. I could sense her sadness from the way she was slumped in her chair. But there was also more than a dash of anger aimed at us for being late. I knew that later we'd be getting a word-a-day for lateness from her.

We quickly did a roll call. Only one—Ali Danzig—was missing. Jen Blackmun, who was a close friend of hers, said that she had chipped a cap and had to go to the dentist. After our first meeting with the group, weeks back, we had divided the remaining volunteers and seen them separately, so there were five or six that neither of us had met before.

We started with the group that had been there with Tanya. Could they identify the woman who had run out? Had she said anything? Of the four who had been there—one had gone out to pick up a pizza—only one, Ellen Sprague, had seen anything.

"She rushed out. Hit the door like she was fleeing a fire."

"Was she saying anything?" I asked.

"Yes," said Brooks Shelby, who was seated next to Ellen.

"What was it?"

"It was…a word or two that she just kept repeating."

"What were they?"

"I couldn't make them out."

"I agree with Brooks. It was only a word or two. It was almost as if she was saying them to herself."

"When a woman comes in, do you have a form that she fills out? Name, phone number, that kind of thing."

"We do. Always," said Jocelyn Marsh, a tall woman with short red hair.

"Could we see that?" asked Alex.

"I'm sorry," said Ellen Sprague, "but we've looked for it—really looked for it—and just couldn't find it."

We kept on for another thirty minutes, mainly asking variations of what we started out with. The only thing we picked up was that one of the volunteers thought she had seen her before. But that, too, led nowhere. When we walked out, we asked Kitty if she wanted a lift to the station house.

"I have my car. But I have some ideas that I'd like to talk to you about. Let's say tomorrow at eleven. I have a ton of stuff to get through first."

"We'll see you then," said Alex.

"Will we get your word-a-day for lateness tomorrow?" I asked.

"You'll get a lot more than that."

When I got home, there was an e-mail from Molly: "Sweet Danny—I really think the test went well. They'll let me know in a week or so. I know they're looking at three other actresses. All with a lot of experience. One I saw recently on *Mad Men*. She's very good. Hope they're looking for a real fresh face. I wanted to call you earlier, but the battery on my cell was real low. I like a lot of things out here, but there are a lot that I don't like. Number one, two, and three is the DRIVING! No one walks. This is a city in search of a city. The only time people look at each other is at a red light. Boy, do I miss you. Do you miss me? I both hope so and more than sort of think so. You know the latest Angel murder even got attention out here. Saw your Inspector Larson on the tube. You look a lot better. I'll be heading back tomorrow. I love it that you'll be picking me up at the airport. I'm actually more nervous about the lunch this Sunday with your family than I was about the test. I can't wait to see you and hold you. Love and much more, Molly."

CHAPTER FIFTY-SEVEN

THE FOLLOWING morning LaVelle came in just after ten, a large shopping bag in her hand.

"For my favorite detectives." She handed the bag to Alex. "You'll love this, and so will the other blue boys in the precinct. Two dozen cupcakes from Big Pony's Shake and Bake on Learsy. Nobody can touch his cupcakes. Icing as thick as a baby's wrist."

"Thank you, LaVelle. Would you like some coffee?"

"Did my cup an hour ago."

"You said you might have some information for us."

"I think I do, Detective Larch. Do you think we could go into one of those offices over there? It feels a little too open here." We walked her into one of our swing offices and closed the door. "That's better. But before I go on, I'm going to ask you for a little help."

"Tell us what you need, and I assure you, LaVelle, that we'll try to help. But first give us what you know."

"I heard on the street that a young working girl ran out of the outreach program. The young lady you're probably interested in is named Dacron Williams. She's young—eighteen or nineteen—and has been on the street for just a month or two."

"Where can we find her?" asked Alex.

"That's the problem. She's gone. Probably back in Philly. That's where she's from. Why'd she run like a dog with a tail on fire? Her friend Chenna, also from Philly, told me she saw someone at the center who had tried to hurt her a few days before."

"Did she say who that was?"

"No. I don't think Dacron knew his name."

"Where can we find Chenna?" I asked.

"I'll come in with her tomorrow. She's also young. She'd feel more relaxed if I was with her. Now, are you ready for my little piece of business?"

"Let's hear it," said Alex. "By the way, these cupcakes are good."

"I knew you'd like them. When I open my coffee place, I'm going to sell Big Pony's stuff. Let me know if you want more of them. I get a discount. A big one."

"Let's get back to your issue, LaVelle," I said.

"Thanks, Detective Martell. A couple of weeks ago, I had to see my sister. She lives in New Haven. That's where I'm from. Well, she had an operation for a lady's problem. She needed some help. So I drove there. Since I don't have a car, I borrowed one from a friend."

"Your friend's name?" asked Alex.

"Metellus."

"Metellus what?"

"Rayburn."

"Isn't he also called MetBoy?"

"Sometimes."

"We've had some dealings with her friend. Right, Danny?"

"Coke and assault, I believe."

"That's in the past. He's straight now. Well, when I came back here a couple of days ago, I made a mistake with a stop sign."

"That doesn't sound very serious," I said.

"You're right. That wasn't it. When the officer did his check, he found out that the car was…stolen."

"That's a problem. A big one."

"You see, I didn't steal it and Metellus didn't steal it. He borrowed it from a cousin. He just forgot to tell him he was taking it. Understand what I'm saying?"

"I think we do, LaVelle," I said. The only thing is, will the judge understand? We have an appointment in a few minutes. What you have to do for us is write down the cousin's name and address and when and where you were pulled over. We'll try to help you."

LaVelle gave us both a hug and promised more, many more, cupcakes.

Larson was in Kitty's office when we walked in. We told them what we picked up from LaVelle. Of course, we also gave them cupcakes.

"Who could she have seen there that would have caused her to run out of the room?" Larson asked. His tone was loud and pissed.

"That's the big one," said Alex.

"What the fuck do you think?"

We looked at each other, and, with the slightest nod from Alex, I jumped in.

"Our guess is that it was someone from outside the outreach room. She probably was rattled when she walked in."

"Then why was Tanya Bohlen targeted? How did someone from outside know that Bohlen interviewed her? This is what we're going to do: First off, I'll call Philly and ask them to do everything they can to find this Dacron. She's the only one who really has the answer. I'm also putting five teams, including the two of you, on the street to interview every hooker who's out there. Scare them, scream at them, do whatever you have to. We need to find this Dacron. She's the key. I got a call this morning from the mayor," he said, his voice dropping a bit. "The media is on his ass big-time, and now he's on mine. You don't want to know what he's threatening to do here."

Without a goodbye, Larson got up and walked out of the office.

"Jesus, I've never seen him like that. This is bad," I said.

"You know we've been humping this thing from the start," said Alex. "With deals like this, you need luck. How many years did it take the Seattle police to nail the Green River guy?"

"I don't know if they ever did," I said.

"He was nailed, but it took them an awful long time to do it."

"Time to change subjects. I got a call last night from Jimmy Warden. He's up in Lakeville, Connecticut. Been there since Saturday. He thinks he's onto something that could tie in to our Angel. He'll be back in a couple of days. I'll set up a meeting for early next week."

CHAPTER FIFTY-EIGHT

"**WHAT DO** you mean I can't have breakfast? It's Sunday. Sunday means bacon and eggs and a toasted bagel buried under cream cheese."

"You'll understand when you sit down at my uncle Sal's restaurant this afternoon. A piece of toast is too much to eat before our family lunch."

Molly didn't like it, but she was so up from her LA trip that she answered by just kissing me on the forehead. Aside from a few telephone calls, we spent the morning sharing the couch and reading the papers. Before we left, Molly told me she was nervous.

"Now go through who'll be there, again."

"This is not a part you're playing. Nothing to memorize here. Just relax. They're all going to like you. Remember, you already have two fans in my uncle and grandmother."

When we got to the restaurant, the whole tribe was there. The family quickly lined up to greet her. Molly got kisses, both cheeks, from everyone. I wanted to sit next to her, but my mother took over and placed Molly between her and my aunt Minnie. My father (my new buddy) sat next to me, arm draped over my shoulder, with Uncle Sal on the other side. My kid brother was there with his lady, Val, who now sported a large engagement ring. Jimmy was still in Connecticut, and Alex had told me he couldn't make it. Everyone else was family. Because the chef was out with a cold, my cousin Teddy was doing the cooking. He had a restaurant in Cranston that served "French" food. That bothered Uncle Sal the same way my father was unhappy with my not joining his law firm. There were about twenty of us at the main table and another dozen at the "kids'" table. Just as the dishes for the first course were being served, my father clinked his glass and stood up.

"I want to propose a toast to a first-time member of our monthly family gathering. This is a very talented woman who I believe we'll be seeing on our TVs very soon. I say she's talented because we saw her perform. The play was called *The Changeling*, and it was written, I think, around the time of Shakespeare. I didn't understand all of the lines, but take my word for it—Molly was great. You know, people in show business are superstitious. You're not allowed to wish them good luck. But I don't think Molly needs luck. The reason for that is she really has talent. Thanks for joining us, Molly Juste, and here's to you."

He raised his glass. We all followed.

"Thank you, Mr. Martell," she said as she stood up. "It's an honor to be here. And thank you, Danny, for inviting me. He told me about your monthly lunches, and now that I'm here, I'm ready to *mangia!*"

The family loved it and actually applauded her. As usual the courses kept coming. Teddy was every bit as good as the Martelli chef. After almost three hours, we left, a clutch of family phone numbers in Molly's hand.

"Danny, I loved it. You have a great family. And what a meal. If I had a role where I had to waddle, I wouldn't have to rehearse it."

I had promised Molly that I would go with her to the museum at Rhode Island School of Design. There was a new show there of sixteenth-century religious paintings she had to look at for a course she was taking at Brown.

"It's not a big show. Maybe twenty paintings, so it won't take long."

The show was great. Most of the paintings were quite small, half of them done on wood. They were mainly of Mary and the Christ Child, but one really caught my eye. It showed Mary with Jesus in her lap and five angels above. All had wings, and they held a crown above Mary's head.

"Danny, you've been staring at that painting for a couple minutes. We have to move on."

When we left, I drove Molly back to her place.

"Am I going to see you later?" she asked.

"What do you think? I'm going home to watch the game. I'll call you when it's over."

I didn't drive home. I went back to the museum. I had to see the painting again. It was by a Jan Provost, 1465–1529. The angels were wrapped in robes. Their robes and wings were different colors. The colors matched our Angels' exactly.

CHAPTER FIFTY-NINE

KITTY CALLED me the next morning. Talk about early…she woke me up!

"Danny, I'm heading into my office. Jimmy's on his way in from Connecticut. He'll be in by eight. Be here. I called Alex. He'll be here, too."

Alex was waiting for me in Kitty's office.

"What the fuck is going on?"

"It's something Jimmy turned up in northwest Connecticut."

"Those killings you told me about from ten years back?"

"Yeah. But he's picked up something new."

Kitty walked in with Jimmy.

"Get up, guys. We're going into Larson's office."

When we walked in, Larson was on the phone. He motioned for all of us to sit down. The chairs were set in a semicircle around his desk.

"Okay," he said when he hung up, "it's your show, Jimmy."

He quickly gave us a recap of the murders that had occurred in northwest Connecticut ten years before. How the murders had stopped after four. It was all stuff that I knew.

"The sheriff's department there worked hard on them but couldn't come up with anything. They did everything we would have done. But I got lucky. My big break came when I stumbled on a connection between the victims. There's a very well-known prep school there called Hotchkiss. One of the victims worked in the office. Another had a brother who taught there. And a third worked as an au pair for one of the deans. I then checked out everybody who worked there during the period of the murders. And I came up with something." Jimmy stopped there. He reached for his coffee and took a sip. I'm not going to say we all held our breath, but no one said a word. "I had asked Danny to give me the list of all the volunteers who worked at the outreach center. And on it I found a name that Danny and Alex know: Brooks Shelby. He taught art history at the school during that time. Here's the topper: his brother, Miles, also taught there. Phys ed and coach of the lacrosse team. They left the school five months after the last killing."

"Jesus," said Alex.

"I have some more. They still own a house there. And they have a car that's registered in Connecticut. Can you guess the make?"

"A Caddy," I said.

"Color?"

"Black, of course," said Larson.

"When I checked what volunteers were there when the hooker ran out, your friend Brooks Shelby's name was on the sign-in sheet."

Larson looked at us.

"What do we do?"

"I want to put their place—"

"They have a house on Benefit," said Jimmy.

"—under surveillance immediately and get a search warrant," Kitty told Larson.

"There's damn little chance we can get a warrant here. We certainly could get a judge to sign one in Connecticut. But I don't want that. I want them tried here in Providence. After we nail their asses here, Connecticut can do whatever they want with them. Right now, we have no direct proof against them for our business. So surveillance is the only route we have," said Larson.

"Also, let's eyeball them where they work. Jimmy, do you know where the brother works?"

"He owns a gym near the Biltmore. Have any of you ever seen him?"

"I did. He was in a play with my friend Molly. He looks like his brother, but he's much bigger. More like the Hulk on steroids."

"Does he look like the kind of guy that could carry a body up a tree?" asked Larson.

"He looks like he could carry a piano."

CHAPTER SIXTY

THE NEXT morning, Kitty told us that she and Larson had decided to put 24/7 surveillance on both of the Shelbys. At their house and at work.

The first four days produced zip. The brothers put in long hours at their jobs. They left together in the morning with Miles driving. He dropped off Brooks and then headed to his gym. Miles didn't leave there until eight thirty or nine. Same for Brooks; even later if he was curating a show. Miles picked up his brother, and they sometimes stopped at a supermarket before heading home.

At the house we sat in our own cars, front and back. Danny and I pulled the nights twice. The shiny new Caddy just sat in the driveway. On day five Kitty informed us that we should stop watching both the house and their places of business.

"They're not grabbing these women during the day. I'd bet my 401(k) that two to six a.m. is when they find their ladies. We'll just watch the house."

Alex and I did four out of the next seven nights. Nothing. We started by following them from work back to their house. The brothers went out to a restaurant twice and once to a movie. They didn't use their car. They walked.

Sunday I slept until three thirty. I didn't have to work until noon the following day, and I had a ton of errands to do. I was getting ready to go to the dry cleaner when the doorbell rang.

"Got a few minutes, Danny?"

It was Kitty, standing there with Larson.

"Sure. Come on in. Want some coffee?" I said and led them into the living room.

"Thanks, but we don't have a lot of time."

"What's up?" I asked as we sat down.

"I think you should start, Catherine," said Larson.

"What I'm going to say, Danny, is not off the record, it's way off the record. Only the three of us can ever know about this conversation. Actually this is a conversation that never took place. Do you follow me?"

"Sort of. But I can guarantee that you really got me interested."

"We've been watching the Shelbys now for eleven days and haven't come up with spit. We tried Judge Torres for a search warrant. No dice. We totally believe that the Shelbys did it. Do you, Danny?"

"Absolutely."

"Well, we're real scared that they'll pull a number like they did in Connecticut. Pick up and go somewhere else. If they split we have no way to reel them in."

"What else can I do aside from what Alex and I have been doing? By the way, do you want me to call him and tell him to come over?"

"No. We only want to talk to you. And there's another reason we came over here. We didn't want to have this talk at the station."

"We've never done this before, and I hope we never have to do this again," said Larson. "We want you to do something that's illegal."

"Danny, we have to get into that house," said Kitty. "And the only way we can do that is to have someone break in."

"Me?" They were both silent. "You want me to do a B and E on the Shelbys' house?"

"It doesn't have to be you, Danny. You know a lot of kids up on the hill. Kids who do this kind of stuff all the time. One of them breaks in, gets away, and then you call the station. We'll have a full team ready to go in. All we need is a couple of hours, tops. Between tossing the place and having our forensic people do their thing, we're sure we'll find what we need. We won't call the Shelbys at work because—wink, wink—we don't have their numbers, so we won't be able to contact them until they get home. And then we'll tell them the sad news about the burglary and, hopefully, cuff them."

"There's one thing wrong with your plan. A big thing."

"What's that?"

"If I bring in a kid to do this, we'll always have a time bomb out there ready to go off. If he decides to talk for any reason, the brothers will be able to walk, and my ass will be grass. There's only one way your plan will work." Both Kitty and Larson stared at me. They weren't smiling. "I'll have to do it."

We worked out that we'd meet again the following morning at my house to wrap things up. As they left, Larson stopped at the door. He put his hand on my shoulder.

"As we said before, Danny, no one will ever know about this. But we will, and we'll always owe you a lot. And so will the city of Providence."

It was almost six by the time I got back home. I wasn't there five minutes when I heard the door open.

"Danny! It's me. You here?"

I went down the stairs two at a time.

"I thought you'd be at the restaurant," I said as I pulled Molly into my arms.

"You're right, but I'm not going to be there tonight. Or tomorrow. Or for the next two or three weeks."

"What do you mean?"

"I'm going to LA," she said, smiling.

"When?"

"My friend Delia, from the restaurant, is outside. She's driving me to the airport. Danny, it's unbelievable. Barry, my agent, called. They sure don't move quickly in TV, but the good news is that I got the part. Four episodes!"

"When will you get back?"

"In a couple of weeks. They're going to shoot two now and the other two in a month. So I won't be gone that long."

"It'll seem long to me," I said and kissed her.

A car horn beeped twice.

"That's Delia. She's watching the clock. I'm going via Chicago this time. They're flying me business class again." She kissed me. Hard this time. "I'll call you when I get to LA."

I walked her to the street. Said hi to Delia and then watched the car drive away. Suddenly the Shelbys and the whole Angel business seemed very far away.

CHAPTER SIXTY-ONE

KITTY AND Larson came to my house at noon the next day. I had called Alex in the morning and told him I wouldn't be riding with him because I had a cold.

"Danny," said Kitty as she sat down, "this is going to take a little time. Any chance we can have the coffee we turned down yesterday?"

I had the coffee brewing, so I was back in a couple of minutes. I brought it out with biscotti that I had gotten the day before.

"I love these things, Danny," Larson said as he scarfed down his third biscotto. "You get these on Federal Hill?"

"When you want the Wailing Wall, you go to Jerusulem; when you want biscotti, you head to Federal Hill."

For the first few minutes, we talked about Angelo Tonnchi. Everyone was talking about Angelo. He was a detective second grade in the Fourth Precinct. A solid guy who had caught a bullet in the shoulder in a shoot-out at the Mercantile Bank a couple of years before. About a week ago, he had announced that he was going to have a sex change. Talk about dropping a bomb.

"Do you know what his—I mean her—name will be?" asked Kitty.

"That's a no-brainer," I said. "Angela."

"Wrong. She's going to be called Michelle. Turns out Tonnchi's a great Obama fan."

We talked about the timing. We all wanted to move fast, but there was a problem. That was Wally Kirshbaum. Wally headed the department's forensic unit and was out for at least another couple of days with strep throat.

"I don't want us to go in without Wally leading his team," said Larson.

"I agree," added Kitty. "The tossing of the place can be done by any number of our guys, but what we're looking for is DNA evidence. For that we really need Wally."

"So we're talking about Wednesday at the earliest. Probably Thursday," said Larson.

"What time do you want me to get into the house?"

"They always leave about nine, no later than nine thirty. Let's say ten thirty."

"I'm thinking of going in through the back door. Small chance of being seen. I'll use a screwdriver. Fast and crude. How do I call it in when I'm finished?"

"You don't," said Larson. "Just figure our team will be there by eleven. If any of them asks, you saw a perp running away from the house. When you checked things out, you saw the back door jimmied open."

"Will Alex be part of the team?"

"Do you want him to be?" asked Kitty.

"I don't think so. I don't want to explain to him why I was in the neighborhood at that time. Whatever I say, I'm pretty sure he wouldn't buy it."

When they left I went upstairs to check my e-mails. Molly was so busy that we hadn't e-mailed since she left. But, happily, there was one from her: "Danny Dear—Writing this at 4:20 a.m. Why? That's obvious. Can't sleep. We shoot today. My part is very good. I'm going to make you cry. I'll be shooting tomorrow, too. This is a two-camera show (see, I'm learning!). Next week I work 3 days. All the shooting is in the studio. Today we shoot at the farmers' market. I'm nervous as hell, but I love it. But boy do I miss you. Finish shooting next Friday at 6. Booked a flight at 9:10. Stops in St. Louis. Providence is not the best place to fly in or out of. Get in at the ungodly hour of 5:25 a.m. Don't expect you to meet me. How about me heading directly for your place? I'll be real quiet. You won't even hear me get into bed. xxxx, M."

Wally Kirshbaum was feeling fine by Tuesday, so we went the next day. The back door popped real easy, and I went in, pulled out a kitchen chair, and waited for the boys.

Wally showed up with a team of four, and Hank Benson came with five tossers. They parked two blocks away and came to the house one by one. The guys moved quickly and efficiently through the house. Kitty and Larson had instructed them to leave no sign of their work. I stayed with Benson's crew, and they came up with nothing. Wally's team checked all the floors from the basement to the attic. Anything that looked like a stain, they swabbed. They vacuumed the carpets and checked the sinks and tub for anything that looked suspicious. They wouldn't be sure there was anything there until they ran their tests, but Wally was real pessimistic.

"I'd bet a lot this place turns out to be clean. Real clean."

I called Kitty before we left and filled her in.

"Shit. I don't believe it. Where are you now?"

"Still in the place."

"Can you get the door to look like nothing happened?"

"I think so. It opened real easy, and I didn't damage the jamb."

"Well, do it. And give the place a close walk-through. It can't look like anyone was there. If the Shelbys get suspicious, they'll do what they did in Connecticut. Split."

"Anything else?"

"You're sure you weren't seen?"

"Positive."

"Great. Just have everybody leave the way they came in. I'd like to see you and Wally when you get in. By the way, are there any other structures on the property?"

"Like a guesthouse or garage?"

"Yes. Anything."

"Just a carport at the end of the driveway. And we checked that, too."

Larson was in Kitty's office when we got there. We went over our morning at the Shelbys' again. Our answers were unfortunately the same: nothing.

"Guys, we're really worried that these creeps will pick up on something we're doing and take the highway," said Larson. "Jimmy Warden just found out that their house in Connecticut has been sold. We were ready to try to get into that place, too. We thought maybe they did their prep work there and then drove them up here. We've got to remember that these guys are smart. Better educated than any mutt we've ever run into. They haven't made and won't make the dumb mistakes we're used to seeing."

"We're going to go back to twenty-four/seven tailing," said Kitty. "We want every car on duty swapped on the hour. We can't let them catch on. We're going to follow them everywhere. Aside from them getting the ladies, they needed time to do the makeup, wings, all of that they couldn't do in a car. We have to find the place where they dressed their Angels."

"What about the brother's gym?" asked Wally.

"We checked that. It closes at midnight, but there's a guy in the lobby all night. And the museum where Brooks works has two night watchmen," said Kitty.

"Is there anything in their background that could help us?" I asked.

"They're clean as a whistle," said Larson. "Not even a speeding ticket. Brought up in Wellesley. Father was a stockbroker. Mother taught at a country-day school. Both went to Williams. Father made a lot of money, and the boys have enough to do anything they want. Danny, we want you and Alex to be the leads full-time on our surveillance team. No one knows this case as well as the two of you. Are you okay with that?"

"The idea is fine. But I think Alex can head it up by himself."

"Why can't you work with him on it?"

"I want you to assign me to my wife's murder. I haven't spoken to either of you about it, but I now believe that you and Jimmy Warden were right about it from the start. You both thought that Linda wasn't murdered by the Angel Killer. I think you're right. And I want to get Jimmy to work with me on it."

Kitty and Larson looked at each other for what seemed like a long time, before Kitty said, "Danny, I completely know where you're coming from on this. Give the inspector and me a little time to talk it over. Believe me, it won't take long. Until we talk to you again about it, work together with Alex on the surveillance. Okay?"

"Sure, as long as it doesn't take too long."

"You have our word on it," said Larson.

CHAPTER SIXTY-TWO

THE NEXT day Alex and I put in thirteen hours, the following a bit over fourteen. I was beginning to feel punchy.

I left a message on Kitty's machine: "When will you and Larson let me know about what I want to do? Want to get on to it ASAP. Spoke to Jimmy. He's ready to work with me."

Alex and I were almost finished with day three (only twelve hours) when I got a call from Kitty: "Danny, I want you and Alex to get in here as soon as you're relieved. Something big has come up."

When I got to Kitty's office, Alex was already there. He was slouched in a chair and needed a shave. So did I.

"What's up, Captain?"

"Remember Dacron?"

"Of course. The hooker who won the hundred-yard dash."

"You got it, Alex. Our friends in Philly have found her." She slid a piece of paper across the desk. "She's staying with her aunt. Do you think you two could drive down there and have a chat with her? Contact Detective Chin. He'll set it up—say, early tomorrow morning. I'd say it's about a four-hour drive."

"Sounds a lot better than sitting in a car and waiting for nothing to happen," said Alex.

"Also pick up an envelope from Jeffers at the desk. It has photos of all the outreach volunteers. There's also one of Miles Shelby, for obvious reasons."

We set out for Philly the next morning at six thirty. We used my car, but I asked Alex to drive. I've never met anybody who likes to drive more than he does. We spent the first hour listening to NPR, then turned it off and talked about the Sox and Alex's latest war-game battle: the Battle of the Somme. We stayed off the Angel business because we both had had enough of it. An hour from Philly, I asked Alex if he didn't mind my shutting my eyes for a bit, and when I opened them, he was parking in front of the station house where we were meeting with Detective First Class Jimmy Chin. We met him in the conference room. Chin had an unusual look for a Chinese guy: he was tall. Real tall. An easy six four.

"Instead of you two following me," he said when we met him inside, "I'll drive you there. The girl's only a couple of miles from here."

As he drove, Chin filled us in. Our young lady was actually born with the name Dacron. Her mother's name was Chenille, and the aunt she was staying with was Denim. This was a family that was really into fabric. Dacron had been picked up twice for soliciting. No time spent inside. She said she was twenty-two, but she was really nineteen.

"How'd you find her?" Alex asked.

"The usual. We worked the street. Though she doesn't seem to be hooking now, we found one who remembered that she sometimes stayed with her aunt."

"I'm surprised she's willing to talk with us."

"One of her raps is still outstanding. It just took a little pressure. She's scared, but she'll talk."

Dacron's aunt lived in a small one-story house in the middle of a street that had seen better times. She answered on the first knock and led us into the living room. All the furniture was covered in plastic. Alex and I sat on the couch, which made sounds like chalk on a blackboard when we shifted our weight.

"Dacron," said Detective Chin, "as I told you yesterday, Detectives Larch and Martell are on the Providence police force.

What they want to talk to you about will in no way put you in any jeopardy of a criminal charge. They just want information from you. Understand?"

Dacron was a pretty girl with a small, round face. She nodded and then looked down. I took a microcassette recorder out of my jacket pocket, turned it on, and put it down on a table. Dacron looked at it as if I had placed a snake there.

"We use that so we don't have to take notes. Nothing you say will be used against you," I told her. "I'm going to show you some photos of people who work at the outreach center. I know you saw someone there that caused you to run out of the room. Look through them carefully, and tell me if you see that person." I handed her the photos. She looked through them slowly. And then, with almost a shudder, she handed me the photo of Brooks Shelby.

"Why did seeing him scare you?" I asked. And then she started to cry. It was soft and lasted only a few moments. "Are you okay?"

She nodded and then spoke with her eyes closed.

"It was late. Maybe three or three thirty. I was on Gano Street by the river. There were only a couple of other girls working. I was at the end of the street by myself. I was getting ready to go to my room, when this car pulled up. New Caddy. The guy asked me if I would go home with him. I told him I only worked from my place. He then said he'd pay me two big. I never ever got that much. So I got in the car. He wasn't a scary-looking guy. Even looked a little gay. Didn't think there could be a problem. He drove over to a small house on Elmgrove. When he pulled into the driveway, the back door opened, and this huge guy started to get in. He reached over to grab me. But what he got was my wig. Big, blond beauty. Just bought it the week before. Cost me ninety bucks. Made me look just like Beyoncé. I was able to open the door and get out. Luckily I was wearing my flats. Ran like a bitch. The big guy was right behind me. He was big, but he could run. But I was on the track team in junior high. After a couple of blocks, he gave up. When I got to the avenue, I found a cab. Real lucky, because just then I saw the black Caddy turn on the avenue. They were looking for me."

We spent another hour going over Dacron's story. There were a few key things we wanted to pin down. One was the house. What did it look like? (One story or two? Color?) What streets was it between? (She was pretty sure it was off of Lloyd.) What did she say to Tanya Bohlen? (Just that she needed the name of a gynecologist.) Did she tell Tanya anything about Brooks Shelby? (No. Once she saw him, she just ran out.)

Before hitting the road again, we decided to have lunch. Chin couldn't join us, but he gave us the name of the best cheesesteak place in town.

"Did she give you enough to move your case along?" he asked after he dropped us off.

"We have some work to do," said Alex, "but I think she gave us the key."

Kitty wanted us back as soon as possible, so we ate the cheesesteaks in the car.

"First thing we have to do is find the house," I said between bites. I had never had a cheesesteak before, and it lived up to what I had heard about it.

"Do you think our girl Dacron will come back voluntarily if we need her?"

"Doubt it. But we won't need her until the trial. Either the boys rent or own the house on Elmgrove. It shouldn't take us long to find out."

"Why do you think they killed Tanya Bohlen?"

"There's only one answer for that. They thought that Dacron told her more than she did."

CHAPTER SIXTY-THREE

IT DIDN'T take us long to locate the Shelby house on Elmgrove. In fact, it was the next day. Frieda, one of our clericals, found it by looking up the real estate sales that had been made on that street in the past two years. Sixteen months earlier, a house at 372 Elmgrove had sold for $417,500 to MABS, LLC. You didn't have to be Sherlock Holmes to figure out that MABS stood for "Miles and Brooks Shelby." Just to make sure, Frieda also checked the electric company and the real estate tax office. Their names were on the bills. We now had enough for Larson to go to Judge Torres for a search warrant. Torres granted it that afternoon at one fifteen, and we were inside with Wally's crew by three.

There was hardly any furniture in the house. But all we needed was in the basement. In a small room next to the oil heater was a long table covered in clear vinyl. There were lots of smears of what looked like makeup. The only window in the room was covered by black electrical tape. The linoleum floor was streaked with colored drips and swirls like a Jackson Pollock painting. A tall metal cabinet against the wall had rolls of the same fabric that was used to make the wings. One shelf had jars of makeup. Two of Wally's team worked the tabletop, while he and another handled the floor. Our guys went through the house, but that took only a few minutes. The closets were bare, and there wasn't a bed in the place. And not that we needed it, but Alex found, in an empty dresser, a folded piece of lined yellow paper. On it, printed in pencil, were the dates and pickup locations for all the victims.

We went upstairs and called Kitty. She wanted Larson on, too, so she said she'd call us back.

"We're both on the line now," Kitty said a few minutes later. "Give it to us."

Alex and I looked at each other, and I nodded to him.

"We got them," he said. "Wally and his gang still have a lot more work to do, but there's definitely a ton of stuff here. But there's a lot more than that. We found makeup and the material that was used for the wings. And, if you can believe it, we found a list of the victims. A list of dates and where they were picked up. This is a slam dunk. When do you want us to pick them up?"

"Come in and meet us in my office. We want to talk this out."

We were in Kitty's office in under ten minutes.

"Kitty and I know what we want to do," said Larson when we sat down, "but we want to hear what you two think. You've been closer to this case than anybody else."

"Alex and I haven't discussed it, but I'm pretty sure we both think the same on this."

"Which is?" he asked.

"We don't want to take the time for a cup of coffee. Let's bring them both in now. Right now."

"At the same time?" asked Kitty.

"It doesn't matter whether we wait for Miles to pick up Brooks and then collar them or do them individually."

"That's what we thought you'd say," said Kitty as she stood up. "Let's do it."

We decided to grab Miles Shelby first. On the way there we called Al Casso, who was handling the watch on him. When we arrived, he was standing in front of the building.

"Anything happening, Al?" Larson asked him.

"Nice and quiet." He opened his notebook. "Our boy Miles arrived at three past ten and hasn't left the place. As usual, he dropped the brother off first. Eddie Pratt, who's watching him, says things are the same there."

"Well," said Kitty, "let's go."

We stopped at the reception desk and told the young woman there that we wanted to see Miles Shelby. There was no need to tell her we were police. Shelby would find out soon enough.

"He's not here."

At least two of us said, "What?"

"Are you sure?" Kitty finally asked. "Where'd he go?"

She hesitated for a moment; then Larson took out his ID and placed it on the counter.

"We're police. We need to know right now, young lady."

"He said that he had to go to the doctor."

"When was that?" asked Alex.

"Right after lunch. He just walked out."

"Walked out?"

"Yes," she answered, motioning to the door behind her.

We all went out that way at more than a fast walk. In the parking lot next to the building, we saw that the black Caddy was still there.

"He must have gone through that building there," said Larson, pointing to the high-rise, "then straight through the lobby to the avenue."

"Then where?" asked Kitty.

"My bet is he went to where his brother works."

"What could have tipped him off?" asked Alex.

"We might not be able to answer that until we nail both of them," said Kitty.

As we left, Larson told Al Casso to follow us. There was no need for surveillance now, and we might need an extra man.

When we got to the museum, we were very surprised when Brooks Shelby's assistant told us he was in his office.

"Are you sure?" I asked.

"I brought him his lunch a couple of hours ago. He was working at his desk."

"Which one is his office?" asked Kitty.

"The one by the stairs. Who should I say wants to see him?"

Larson flashed his badge again, and we all walked over to the door. We didn't knock. With Larson in the lead, we just walked in. And she was right. Brooks Shelby was at his desk. Or rather, his battered head was lying on it. A small puddle of blood was under his head. Alex took his pulse, which we all knew didn't exist, while Kitty called an ambulance. Now we had only one Angel Killer to look for.

We returned to the precinct to figure out our next move. I called Wally Kirshbaum and filled him in. He said he'd send a couple of his people out to scout around. He called me back a half hour later.

"We found the person who dropped the dime," he said. "Name of Carmel Snead. She's got to be in her eighties. Lives across the street. In a wheelchair. She was paid to watch the house. She saw us when we came over and called Miles. Can't fault her. She was just doing her job. Makes sense that he wanted that place watched all the time."

Before we split for the night, we met again in Kitty's office.

"We spoke with the metro editor of the paper and all the local channels," she told us. "We gave them photos of Miles Shelby. Got them from the gym. Larson is going to be interviewed on the evening news. We got the Litchfield County cops in on it. They're going to watch the Shelbys' house there."

"I thought it was sold," I said.

"It was, but the buyers haven't moved in yet."

"Are you going to keep up the surveillance on the houses and where they worked?"

"We have to, but I don't think we'll see him come near them. He's smart, and he has money. It's not going to be easy to catch this creep."

"Why do you say that?" asked Alex. "His face is going to be all over the place. Somebody will make him."

"He'll dye his hair. He'll be in a good suit. And he's white. Take my word, it's going to take some time. I'll bet a couple of months' pay he's not even in Providence. By the way, I just got the preliminary coroner's report."

"What was Brooks hit with?" I asked.

"Nothing. His head was just banged against the desk. All that blood was from a flesh wound. If that was all, the worst he would have had was a headache. No, he was taken out like one of the Angels. Strangled."

CHAPTER SIXTY-FOUR

When I got home, there was a message from Molly: "Danny Dear—Change in plans! I'll be coming home tomorrow night. Nine forty on Delta two-two-eight. Lots to tell you. All good. But best of all, I'll be seeing you…and holding you."

I knew I had to tell Molly about Shelby. I'd do it right after I picked her up.

The next day was a solid twelver. Alex and I decided to split up. He took the museum where Brooks worked, and I handled Miles's gym. I started at seven and stopped only for a sandwich. There were five full-time people at the gym. All of them were stunned by the news. Miles got high marks as a boss, and all were worried about whether they would still have their jobs. I asked all of them the obvious question: Was Miles particularly close to any of the clients or staff? Negative on that, but I picked up something good enough that I immediately called Kitty on it.

"I think I have something."

"I'm listening."

"One of the employees at the gym told me that Miles had a house on the Cape that he used in the summer."

"Where? The Cape's a big place."

"She thought near Hyannis."

"I'll get some people working on it."

That was the high point of the day. I picked up my list of volunteers at the outreach center and saw five of them before finally calling it a day. Came up empty.

"We found the house on the Cape," said Kitty when I went into her office.

"It's in their father's name. He's in a retirement home. The state troopers went over there an hour ago. For now it's empty. They'll keep a watch on it. But I think he's too smart to head there."

"What do we do now?"

"Keep doing what we're doing and hope he makes a mistake."

Molly's plane got in thirty minutes early, but I got to the airport almost an hour before that. I guess you could say I really wanted to see her. She came off the plane first and almost sprinted into my arms. She looked great. After we untangled, we went to the luggage carousel.

"You look terrific, Actress Lady."

"So do you, Danny Boy, though you look a bit tired."

"As usual, you're very perceptive, and I'll explain why over dinner."

"I'd rather you talk about other things."

"What do you have in mind?"

"Us," she answered and then kissed me again.

We ate at my uncle's restaurant, but I don't remember what we had. Luckily he didn't spend much time at our table because the restaurant was packed. When we finished we went to Molly's apartment. After she looked at her mail, we made our way to the bedroom, where we held each other for a long time.

"I have great news that I'm not so happy about," she said when we came up for air.

The great news really was great. Barry, her agent, expected to get an offer for Molly to do at least ten episodes next season.

"Why are you unhappy about that?"

"You must really be tired, Danny. Don't you get it? I'll be away from you for a long, long time."

"Am I tired or just getting stupid? I feel a little depressed already," I said as I pulled her close to me. "But since you're here now, let's do something that we both like to do."

The next morning, more than a dozen of us met with Kitty in the conference room. She went over everything that was being done. We were in the process of contacting every member of Miles Shelby's family. Most of them lived in the Northeast, but so far no leads. Most were out of touch with him. The police in every state now had Shelby's photo. Airports, bus depots, and car rental agencies had all been alerted. The FBI couldn't get in yet because all the crimes were committed within the state.

"I personally think that he's out of the state. Far out. We have our work cut out. This is a smart guy who's also an actor. He knows makeup and apparently speaks three languages. I'll be handing out to each of you a list of people who had any kind of contact with him. We got the names off of his computer. I'll tell you how tough we think it will be to nail this creep: we've contacted a new show that just started on one of the cable stations. Quite a bit like *America's Most Wanted*. We've pushed them to put Shelby on ASAP. They've had great success with lots of other murder cases. People regularly call in with sightings on stories that they run. Our problem with the show is that they won't be able to run the Shelby segment for at least three months."

"Have we checked that he doesn't own another house here?" asked a detective from the Fourth.

"Yes. The house on Elmgrove is the only one. We're now running a check on apartment leases done in the last two years."

Later, as Alex and I walked to the lot to pick up our cars, he said, "What do you think? Is he still in town?"

"I'd always vote with Kitty. If she thinks he's fled the coop, then I'd bet he has. You?"

"Yeah. I guess so. It's too bad. We've worked our asses off on this one, and someone else is going to grab him."

CHAPTER SIXTY-FIVE

THE FOLLOWING week was relentlessly boring. I questioned people that I knew from the start didn't have a clue where Miles Shelby was. Reports kept coming in from people who "saw" him. Cab drivers, waitresses, hookers (of course), school crossing guards, and au pairs led the way. The media couldn't get enough of the story. Miles Shelby's picture was everywhere. Then, from someone who knew him in Connecticut, we discovered that he wore a rug! When he was a kid, he had been afflicted with alopecia and lost all the hair on his head. Kitty contacted the press, and they started to run his photo without hair. Of course, he probably was wearing a piece. What color or style was anyone's guess.

After a week and a half of working on the Miles hunt, I called Kitty.

"I have to talk to you."

"You have something?"

"No. I just have to see you."

"I'll be through by seven or so. Meet me at Learsy's."

Learsy's was a cocktail lounge in the Four Seasons Hotel. Though Kitty was a dedicated vegetarian, she was also a dedicated drinker. I'd never seen her show any signs of overimbibing, but she really liked her grain and fruit in liquid form.

"I know why you want to see me," she said after taking a sip from a dry martini with three olives. It was a real gin martini with the smallest splash of vermouth. She talked the bartender through it as if she were a air traffic controller instructing a damaged plane how to land.

"Well, when can Jimmy and I start?"

"First off, Danny, are you sure you want to do this?"

"Absolutely."

"I know you have a lady friend. Her name's Molly, right? Have you spoken to her about this?"

"No. I keep her out of my police work."

"Where do you think you and Jimmy are going to start?"

"From the very beginning. The person who almost killed Tutlow is the same one who planted Linda's stuff in his pockets and in his room. That's the guy we have to find."

"Are you sure you want to work with just Jimmy?"

"I don't need anyone else."

"Well this might give you a small head start," she said as she slid a folder across the table.

"What's this?"

"I had Perkins and Granger do some preliminary nosing around a few days ago. They didn't come with much, but they covered a few bases that you won't have to spend time on."

"Like what?"

"Her cell phone. They checked all calls. In and out. Over the last three months. Now it's something you don't have to do. There's a list of them in there."

CHAPTER SIXTY-SIX

WE COULDN'T start the next day because Jimmy had to visit his sister in Boothbay Harbor. She was recovering from back surgery. He'd be back the next day around lunchtime. That gave me time to do something I had put off for a long time: going through Linda's things. I had given away her clothes right after the funeral. Her sister took the mink coat, and I divided her jewelry between her mother and her friends. Now came the hard stuff: I went to her desk and started going through the drawers. There were a lot of letters. I took them out and bundled them with a rubber band. I did the same with her checkbook and bank statements. I found her appointment book in the second drawer with her AmEx, MasterCard, and Visa receipts. There was also an Hermès coin purse bursting with quarters. I then went through the small file cabinet that was next to her desk. That contained mainly business letters and memos. After I put all the stuff on the dining room table, I went up to the bedroom and looked at the two dressers she had used. All the clothes were gone, but I found dozens of photographs and keys. The keys were on three different rings, with one of the rings holding only one key. That was about it.

As I was getting ready to go through her appointment book, I remembered that Linda's office had sent me two large boxes of her stuff right after the funeral. I had put them, unopened, in the garage. I'd bring them in later. It was about a minute after opening the appointment book that I started to cry. First just wet eyes, then big-time sobs. Since I was alone, I went with it. I didn't look at my watch, I just let it happen. And I started to say aloud,

"Linda, Linda, why, damn it, why? Did you have any idea how much you meant to me? I loved you, baby. I really loved you." And soon I was shouting: "I miss you, darling! I always will! I can't lie to you, baby. I really like Molly. That's not right. I love her.

"Not the way I loved you, but it's still love. I keep asking myself if my thing with Molly is wrong. I wish you could tell me it's not. I know we got together pretty soon after you died, but I can't believe that's a bad thing. Oh, I don't know what the fuck I'm saying, baby. Just remember, I still love you."

I don't know how long I sat there. I kept blowing my nose until my handkerchief was soaked. I went to the kitchen and then couldn't remember why I was there. Oh, yeah. A drink. That's what I needed. I went to the fridge and took out the vodka. Whoa! I checked my watch—10:17 a.m. *Pretty fucking early for a drink, Martell.* It wasn't easy, but I put the bottle back. I went to the dining room and picked up her appointment book again. I decided what I had to find out first was what Linda was doing in the days before she was killed. I looked at the preceding week. Lots of meetings, a business lunch almost every day, and not much else. No names I couldn't identify. She did have two drink dates, but all she wrote was, *Drinks/7:30* and, two nights before her body was discovered, *Drinks/Talk/Call First.*

I spent the next two hours on the letters. They were mainly to her mother and sister, and the few that were to friends had nothing in them. I went out to the garage and brought in the boxes from her office. As soon as I opened the first box, stacked to the top with memos, phone logs, expense reports, P&Ls, and copies of articles, I closed it. I knew I wasn't up to it. I left a message for Kitty saying that Jimmy and I were going to start tomorrow and I'd be in touch, and one for Alex asking if he was free for dinner that night. Molly was having dinner with her buddies from the restaurant. Now that she was a working actress making real money, she told her friends that it was her treat.

Alex called me back an hour later. "Can't make it, partner. Have a date. How about tomorrow?"

"That won't work. Molly and I are going to Boston to see a play. Making any progress on the Miles front?"

"I'm beginning to think we'll catch Judge Crater first. Anything on your end?"

"Nada city."

I stayed away from what Jimmy and I were getting into. Kitty thought it best that we keep it to ourselves.

Jimmy came over to my place the next day at ten.

"How's your sister?"

"Tess is using a walker. In a week or two she'll be on a cane. A little less pain every day. Doctor thinks she'll be able to jog in a couple of months. We'll see."

I told him that Kitty had had a couple of our guys check out Linda's cell phone. She thought there wasn't anything there, but I hadn't had a chance yet to check it.

"How do you want to handle things?" he asked.

"Why don't you look at this first," I said, handing him the folder on the cell phone. "Maybe they missed something. I'll put together a list of her friends. There are a few that she was very close to that I should see alone. We can see the rest together. After that we should go to her office. That'll probably be the day after tomorrow. That sound okay to you?"

"You're the boss on this one, Danny. I'm just the helper."

CHAPTER SIXTY-SEVEN

THE NEXT morning I met Jimmy at his place. I was walking up the stairs when the front door opened and Dolores Ricci stepped out. Jimmy was at her side, arm around her waist.

"Hi, Danny," she said. "I keep telling Jimmy that we have to have dinner with you and your lady friend. I don't know if he told you, but we saw her in that play she was in at Brown. She's both very good and very good looking."

"We'd love it, Dolores. Problem is that Molly is going back to LA. She's got a part on a TV show."

"That's right. Your father mentioned it to me."

I looked over to Jimmy. He was smiling at Dolores. I hadn't seen him smile like that in a long time.

"Danny and I have some work to do, baby," he said. "You'll be home the usual time?"

"I have to drop something off at my sister's. Say, seven, seven thirty."

She gave him a quick kiss and headed to her car, parked behind Jimmy's in the driveway.

When we sat down at the kitchen table for a cup of coffee, Jimmy handed the folder containing the cell phone information to me.

"There's nothing here," he said. "Perkins and Granger checked every call. Ninety percent are business, and the rest are calls to either friends and family or the dry cleaner."

"That's good. Now we don't have to hump that. Here's what I mentioned last night," I said as I handed him a list of Linda's friends. There were four names on it. Mine had three, but I knew I would have to spend more time with them. They were Linda's closest friends.

"Before we start, Danny, there's something I have to know."

"What's that?"

"Did you ever find out where Linda was on those nights she didn't come home? How many was it?"

"Two. And no. I never did. That's really what we have to find out. Who she was with before they found her... You know, Jimmy, I don't know why I can't use that word. *Body*. But I can't. Do you understand what I'm saying?"

"I think I do. When Bonnie died, it took me a while—quite a while—to even say the word *dead*. I can't begin to imagine dealing with what you're going through. Seeing Bonnie in pain, dying by fractions each day, was terrible. But to lose her the way you lost Linda, like being slammed in the face and the guts at the same time, is way tougher." He reached across the table and squeezed my shoulder. "You're going to be all right, and we're going to find the guy who did it. Now tell me about the women I'm going to see."

CHAPTER SIXTY-EIGHT

AT THE top of my list were Olivia Bluth and Amanda Laster. Both of them went to grad school with Linda. Olivia lived in town, Amanda in Smithfield. Since Olivia was near, I saw her first. She was pregnant with her second child and, together with her husband, Don, had been fixing up their Victorian since the first time I had met them.

"It's good to see you, Danny," she said as she opened the door. "I don't have a lot of time because I'm interviewing a new nanny in a half hour or so."

"This shouldn't take too long, Olivia."

I followed her into the living room.

"You know, I think of Linda all the time."

I could see where this was going, and I didn't want to go there.

"So do I, but I'm here to talk to you about something else. About a very specific time, just before Linda was murdered. How frequently did the two of you speak?"

"It varied. Sometimes once a week."

"Did you talk to her in the days before she was found?"

"I don't think so."

"Well, when you spoke to her last, how did she sound?"

"Just like the Linda I've always known. Bright, funny, upbeat—"

"Did she confide in you?"

"What do you mean, Danny?"

I knew I had to tap-dance into this softly.

"Do you think she would tell you something she might not tell me?"

"You mean would she tell me a secret? Of course she would. We've done that with each other since we became friends."

"Okay. This isn't easy for me to say. Did she ever mention that she was involved with another man?"

"If she did, I wouldn't tell you. But since she didn't, I can. No. Never. She loved you, Danny. I know you've been through hell, but you can't think that way. She was beautiful in every way, and that's how you should remember her."

I doubt if Olivia called Amanda while I drove to her apartment in Smithfield, but I got the same response from her. Again I heard there was only one man in Linda's life, and that was me.

The last name on my list was Sasha Crane. She had been, hands down, Linda's best friend. They shared an apartment together for two years after college, and she was Linda's maid of honor at our wedding. The next morning, I had trouble starting my car. I called Alex about borrowing his.

"What's wrong with your wheels?"

"Who the fuck knows? Won't start."

"Sure. Use mine."

We worked out that he'd pick me up in the morning, and I'd drop him off at the station. After a very depressing bottle of beer, I started going through one of the cartons from Linda's office. After a half hour I gave that up and went downstairs to work out. I did a full session—cardio, weights, and stretching—and felt a lot better. Before I opened another beer, I called Jimmy.

"Land anything?"

"Not even a guppy. Saw three of the ladies on the list, and all I learned was how great a gal she was and how happy the two of you were. I have one more to see tomorrow, and then what?"

"I have one more, too. We'll talk after we finish."

Alex called me the next morning. He was in a rush and couldn't pick me up. He said he'd leave his car in the station's parking lot with the keys in the visor. I walked about ten blocks to a diner on Parker, where Sasha was waiting for me in a booth at the back. She had recently been divorced (her second) and worked as a tax accountant in the building next to where Linda had worked. She was an attractive woman who would be a knockout if she dropped twenty pounds. I kissed her on the cheek and sat down.

"You look terrific, Sasha."

"So do you, Danny. I hear you have a new friend."

"Where'd you hear that?"

"Your father." Of course—my dad and Sasha tossed business back and forth to each other all the time. "She sounds very nice."

"She is, but I'm here to talk about Linda."

Sasha pulled a handkerchief out of her handbag and dabbed at her eyes, which were suddenly wet.

"I miss her so much, Danny."

"So do I." She reached across the table and clasped my hand. After a moment, I eased my hand away. "Did you speak with Linda at the very end?"

"What do you mean by 'the very end'?"

"Just before she was found."

"I don't remember. I might have."

"In the days before they found her, was she staying with you?"

"No."

"Are you sure?"

"The last time she stayed with me was before the two of you got married."

I had asked Sasha the same thing when I couldn't find Linda. I had believed her then, and I believed her now.

I wrapped it up with her fifteen minutes later. I knew then that I wouldn't find out from her who Linda was with before she was killed.

I took a cab to the station. Alex's car was there in the front of the lot. I got in and took my phone out of my pocket to call Jimmy. And then I decided I'd call him from my place. Though Alex and I were about the same height, he liked to keep the seat a lot closer to the steering wheel. I reached down to move the seat back, when something jabbed into my index finger. Jesus, it hurt. Blood was dripping from it. I opened the door and got out. I crouched down to see what had done the damage. It was a pin. A gold oval with a rose engraved on the front. I turned it over, though I didn't have to. I knew that it was Linda's. There on the back were her initials and a date: Linda's birthday. And below that the word *Always*. I had given it to her three years before. She had cried when I pinned it on her.

CHAPTER SIXTY-NINE

I **DROVE** home and dropped the pin on the kitchen table and just stared at it. My cell rang. It was Molly. I didn't answer it. Then it rang again. It was Jimmy. I didn't answer it either. I wanted a drink in the worst way, but I knew that was not the path to take. I tried to figure out what was exploding inside me. Anger? No. That was a small-time, chickenshit feeling. I was way beyond that. Rage? That felt closer, but it didn't really work either. The right term was *murderous rage*.

Don't fuck around, Martell. Say it! You want to kill Alex... slowly and painfully. Murder the fucker. But you're not going to do that. Why? Because your ass will wind up in prison. For a long, long time. What you should do is call Jimmy. He'll know what to do. But you're not going to do that either, are you? What you're going to do is call Alex.

"Hi, it's Danny."

"What's up, partner?"

"I have to see you."

"You found something on the Angel business?"

"Yeah."

"Great."

"When can we get together?"

"I'm tied up all day, but we can meet for a drink later. Say, six."

"How about your place?"

"Tonight's my war-gaming night. The place is filled with tables and hundreds of soldiers. I don't want to knock anything over. We're only a session away from finishing this battle."

.

"Don't worry about your battle. I'll be careful. See you at six."

The landline rang several times, but I didn't pick it up. When I checked later, there were three messages: my mother wanting to know if I could come over for dinner that night; Kitty asking how we were doing; and Molly saying that not only had they picked her up for twelve episodes, but her agent had gotten her a part in a movie. It was a week's work playing Paul Rudd's half-sister in a comedy. She had to leave for that in three days. Not to LA, but to Vancouver. I left a message on her phone that I was busy and would call her tomorrow.

It was almost five when I finally picked up the pin off the table. I went to the desk in the study and took out an envelope. It had Linda's name and address on the back flap. The type was raised. She had bought the stationery at Tiffany. I put the pin in and sealed it. I dropped it into my jacket pocket.

I went to the phone twice to call Jimmy, but I stopped before punching in his number. If I told him about the pin, he would have said we had to see Kitty. She'd have Alex brought in and worked over. He wouldn't give us anything, but eventually we'd find something. That would be the smart thing to do. Smart wasn't the avenue I wanted to travel down.

As with most cities, cops in Providence are required to carry their guns at all times while they are in the city, whether on duty or not. I took mine out of my shoulder holster and put it in the desk. I smiled. "Danny," I said aloud, "you're not a totally deranged shmuck. You just did the right thing. The piece could only lead to problems. Big ones."

Alex lived about two miles away. I parked on the street in front of his building and waited. I kept reaching into my pocket to touch the envelope. I don't know how long I sat there. A dirty, dented Audi pulled up across the street. It was Applebaum's car. I got out and walked over just as Alex got out.

"Boy, you're an on-time guy," he said as he patted me on the back. "You know, that bar around the corner, Orson's Hat, is pretty good. Generally has some nice ladies around. Why don't we give it a shot?"

"I'm not in the mood for a bar," I said as I handed him his car keys. "And don't worry, I won't knock one little metal guy over."

"Whatever you say, Danny Boy."

I followed him up to his apartment on the second floor. The front door opened onto a large dining room. There were two gateleg tables completely filled with small metal soldiers in different painted uniforms. Since they were fighting the Battle of the Wilderness, the soldiers, gray and blue, were set on a clay base that had been modeled into fields, hillsides, and valleys, studded with small plastic trees and buildings.

We went into the living room, where three more tables were set up. Most of the furniture had been moved out, except for a couple of chairs near the windows that faced onto the street.

"Vodka?"

"Not right now."

"Well, I need one," he said, going to the kitchen. When he got back, I handed him the envelope. "What's this?"

"Open it."

When people open envelopes, they usually open them from the back. So I could see Alex hesitate when he noticed Linda's name. He didn't take out the pin.

"What the fuck is this?"

"Take it out."

"What's this all about, Danny?"

"Take the fucking pin out, Alex," I said, my voice loud enough to hail a cab. He took it out and quickly dropped it back in. "You didn't see the engraving on the back. It belonged to Linda. Remember her?"

"Where are you going with this, Martell?"

"Why don't you ask me where I found it?" Alex took a big swallow of vodka and sat down. "I'm surprised you're not interested. It was in your car. Under the front seat. I gave it to her on her birthday a couple of years ago."

"So?"

"Tell me the story, motherfucker. I want it right now."

"I think you should cool down, my friend."

I jumped up and punched Alex on the side of the head. My fist landed square on the temple, and he fell to the floor. I pulled him up and hit him two or three times in the gut. Then I shoved him across the room, taking out two tables and several hundred troops that flew into the air like popcorn. I didn't know anything about the Battle of the Wilderness, but I doubted that it ended this way. Then I kicked him a few times. Hard. I pinned him to the floor and hit him again and again. I didn't want to put him out, so I stopped. There was blood all over the place. Alex always carried his gun in an ankle holster. I reached down and pulled it out. I tossed it across the room.

"Okay. Tell me what you did to Linda."

"Let me up," he barely got out. "I think you broke a tooth."

"Oh, that's too bad. If you don't tell me the story—the whole fucking story—you won't need any teeth."

"What story?"

I hit him again. This time he went straight down. I heard his nose break.

"I came over here thinking I might kill you. Do you want me to do that?"

"What do you want me to tell you? That I had an affair with Linda? What do you think?" It took a lot not to punch him again.

"How long?"

"Two, three months. I didn't want to, but you know me, Danny. I got the willpower of a slug."

"How did you kill her?"

"You have little reason to, but you have to believe me. It was an accident. Could you ease up on me with your knees? I'm having trouble breathing." I pulled up just a little. "We got into an argument. Big-time. Right in this room. She said she was going to tell you about us. Then she slapped me. Hard. Then she scratched me. You asked me about it the next day. I told you it was a cat… some cat. She came at me again. I was sitting in that chair right over there. Reflexively I just kicked out at her. She flew across the room. Her head landed against the side of that fireplace over there. Made a hell of a sound. I don't know if it was the blow to the back of her head or her neck being broken. But she had no pulse when I finally got over to her.

"I had some photos of the other Angels here. Then I spent some time studying them. Getting the dimensions of the wings. I once had to take a home ec class in high school—never thought I'd use the sewing part."

"And you took out Tutlow, didn't you?"

"Yeah. Another dumb move."

I stared down at the guy who I had once thought of as my best friend. It had been a smart move to leave my gun behind. I stood up and actually reached down to help him.

"This is what you're going to do. Within four days you're going to go in and see Kitty and Larson and tell them the story. Everything. I'd advise you to have a lawyer with you and bail money ready. Certainly at least $250,000. If you don't do it, I will lay it out for them. Understood?" Looking down, he nodded. "Look up, you piece of shit, because this is the last time you'll ever see me." As soon as he looked up, I punched him with all my might. He spun around and crashed into the third table. There would be no war gaming tonight.

Alex went in to see Kitty and Larson two days later. He was arrested in Kitty's office and released on bail of $225,000 the next day. The following week I went in and handed Kitty my letter of resignation. The first person I told was Molly. Then I asked her if she minded if I went to LA and lived with her. She didn't mind at all. My parents were shocked by my decision, but when I told my dad that I was going to take the California bar exam and practice out there, he actually smiled.

AFTER

Silver Lake is a hilly neighborhood east of Hollywood and northwest of downtown Los Angeles. The town circles the Silver Lake Reservoir, which was created in 1906. A jogging path of a little over two miles rims it.

Elise Davis and Joyce Snyder had been running around the reservoir every morning for almost four months since meeting in a yoga class in Echo Park. They lived only two blocks from each other on Redcliff Street, and they liked to run early, always before six thirty, when the path was deserted. They ran the course, doing five nine-minute miles, and talked the whole time. Mainly they talked about marriage (both were divorced), their jobs, and keeping their weight down. Since it was December and the sun didn't rise until a little past seven, they started their run in the dark. Each wore a small flashlight attached by a band that circled her baseball cap.

As they entered mile four, Joyce said, "I think I'd like to stop at four. I drank a little too much last night."

"Fine by me."

"In fact, why don't we stop at that eucalyptus grove just after the turn?"

"That's even better."

As usual they ended by doing a halfhearted sprint the last hundred yards and then collapsed on a grassy bank.

"What's always better than running is stopping," said Elise as she sat up and took a few deep breaths.

"Amen."

"I can't believe how thoughtless some people are," said Joyce as she stood up and walked toward the grove. "Look at that dirty fabric somebody just tossed away. Inconsiderate—"

And then she started to scream. And when Elise got beside her, she started screaming, too. There, lying on the ground in front of them, was not a dirty bundle of fabric but rather a pretty young woman wrapped in purple cotton with what looked like golden wings splayed out behind her. On each wing was stitched in black the Roman numeral *I*. They both pulled out their cell phones, but Joyce tapped out 911 first. They moved away from the body without talking and waited for the sound of the police siren. They didn't know it, but Los Angeles had just been given its first Angel.

ACKNOWLEDGMENTS

I'VE ALWAYS believed that writing a book was like building a house from the inside. You need good people to help you see what it really looks like. For that I want to thank my editor, Alan Turkus, whose steady hand and sharp eye always moved this book forward. And to my agent Phillip Spitzer and his associate, Lukas Ortiz, thanks for your belief and for steering *Angel Wings* in the right direction.

ABOUT THE AUTHOR

Photograph by Madeleine Morel, 2012

BORN AND bred in Brooklyn, New York, Howard Kaminsky attended Brooklyn College, San Francisco State University, and the University of California at Berkeley. The author of seven books, he previously was president and publisher of Warner Books, Random House, and William Morrow/ Avon, and he served on the Board of Directors of American Publishers Association and the National Book Foundation. His screenplays include 1972's *Homebodies*. He coproduced the film *My Dog Tulip* and he is currently producing a documentary, *The Two Popes*, about the man who created the *National Enquirer* and his father. Today he splits his time between New York City and Connecticut, where he is at work on his new novel, *The Perfection Project*.